These Lonesome Hills

LETHA BOYER

CAPPER PRESS
Topeka, Kansas

◆

Published by Capper Press
616 Jefferson, Topeka, Kansas 66607

Cover Illustration and Calligraphy by Catherine Ledeker
Cover Design and Book Design by Kathy Snyman
Edited by Tammy Dodson ◆ Typeset by Karen Gomel

ISBN 0-941678-08-3
First Printing, November 1989
Printed and bound in the United States of America

◆

*These Lonesome Hills was first published as a serialized novel
in Capper's magazine (formerly Capper's Weekly)
from March 12, 1985 through October 22, 1985.*

For more information about Capper Press titles
or to place an order, please call:
(Toll-Free) 1-800-777-7171, extension 107, or (913) 295-1107.

Capper Fireside Library

*F*eaturing
the most popular novels previously
published in *Capper's* magazine, as well as
original novels by favorite *Capper's* authors, the
Capper Fireside Library presents the best of fiction in
quality softcover editions for the family library. Born out of
the great popularity of *Capper's* serialized fiction, this
series is for readers of all ages who love a good
story. So curl up in a comfortable chair,
flip the page, and let the storyteller
whisk you away into the world
of this novel from the
*Capper Fireside
Library.*

Contents

These Lonesome Hills

CHAPTER ONE

The New Teacher

"**I**t's quite beautiful country. So much greenery and so tranquil. Do we have much further to go?"

"Almost there. Look ahead of you and you'll see one of the reasons the teacher has to live-in."

"My goodness! How do we get across? It looks quite deep."

"Right now it's no more than eight or ten inches, but it can get several feet deep when there are heavy rains."

The car slowed to a crawl. The man shifted down to first gear and eased the car into the water. "The bottom is solid rock, so there's no danger of getting stuck," he said. "Willow Creek, better known in these parts as 'Willer Crick.'"

"Haven't they heard of bridges out here?"

"Don't feel they need a bridge since most of them still use a team of mules and a wagon."

"I see."

"Here's your first family."

"You're not serious," I said. I stared in astonishment at the dilapidated shack we were approaching. Several of the windows were broken out, the screen door hung crazily on its hinges, the roof sagged.

As we drew nearer, several ragamuffin children came and stared out through the open doorway, three scrawny mongrel dogs ran out barking.

"The Anderson family," said my companion.

"That house should be condemned. What do they do in winter?"

"Cover the windows with boards, cardboard, whatever they can find. Stuff newspapers in the cracks. Stay huddled around the stove, sleep three or four to a bed."

"How many children?"

"Not sure, I've lost count, about six or seven, I expect. Only three or four of school age."

"Are there many families like that?"

"Several, not all that extreme, of course. Most of these hill people are poor. You'll find a good many of them barefoot on the first day of school, some of them in rags, uncombed, unwashed, sometimes there are problems with head lice. It's not a prosperous area, Miss Davis."

"What is their main source of income?"

"The Anderson family lives on A.D.C.—Aid to Dependent Children, in case you're not up on your welfare services. He's disabled, bad back, or so he says. Some of the men do a little farming, but most of them work at the sawmill farther back in the hills."

"Then surely they make a fairly decent living."

"Most of them make just enough to get by on."

He glanced over his shoulder at me and grinned. "Quite an adventure you've set out on, isn't it, Miss Davis? But that's what you wanted, right?"

"Right," I answered, but my voice sounded a little hollow even in my own ears.

"Not getting cold feet?"

"Oh no, of course not."

"Good."

There was silence in the car as we wound our way around and up and down the gentle, rolling hills. It was a dirt road so Mr. Hooper drove slowly, but still a cloud of dust rose up behind us. I sat thoughtful, aware that he glanced over at me again. Was he having second thoughts about hiring me?

He was superintendent of schools, an older man, white-haired and affable. He'd been reluctant to hire me, but teachers who wanted these isolated country schools were not that plentiful and it was especially hard to find a teacher for this particular school because the teacher had to live-in.

"Mr. Hooper?"

"Yes?"

"The family I'll be staying with, you said their name is Hilton?"

"Clemmy and Willy Hilton."

"Clemmy?"

"For Clementine, I expect."

"Tell me something about them. You said they're an older couple and live in an actual log cabin, but that's all I know."

"No modern conveniences, I told you that, I believe."

"Yes, but—"

"What would you like to know, Miss Davis?"

"I—are they clean?"

"Clemmy is an excellent housekeeper and a great cook. However, Willy may take some getting used to. He loves his hounds and will insist on having some of them inside the house, but Clemmy won't let them in the kitchen. He smokes a pipe, never see him without it. Chews too, though Clemmy won't let him spit on her floors anymore. Makes him carry a coffee can around with him."

"Ugh."

He chuckled.

"There's a son still living at home, at least part of the time. He does some building with a brother who lives in town, but I understand he's mostly doing cabinetmaking now. He has a shop near the house, very modern, with electricity, even."

"I suppose he chews too."

"No, he doesn't even smoke, as far as I know. Davy's a pretty decent sort, known him since he was a boy. He'll help

3

you out if you have any problems with any of your students."

"What kind of problems?"

"Disciplinary problems, Miss Davis. You'll have them. Some of the boys are big overgrown kids, bigger than you are. I let you have this school because I knew Davy would stand behind you. He has a lot of influence with the kids, a good many of them are his nieces and nephews."

"I'm not used to calling on other people to handle my problems, Mr. Hooper."

"But then you've never taught at this kind of school before, have you? If you're going to make a success of it, you'll have to recognize your limitations and not be too proud to ask for help."

He paused and cast another glance in my direction.

"The teacher last year quit four months before the term was over. Put us in quite a bind. I hope you won't do that."

"I'm not in the habit of running out on my commitments."

"It can get pretty lonesome out here."

"I'm not the sort of person who has to have constant companionship."

"That'll help. Well, there's the cabin. What do you think?"

I leaned forward to get a better view. The cabin nestled down in a valley with green hills as a backdrop. It looked weather-beaten and mellow with age. A long, open porch ran the length of the front of the cabin and around to one side. A man sat there in an old rocker, one hand on the pipe in his mouth, the other hand hanging down by his side and resting on the head of a hound.

"The yard was bare, hard-packed dirt with several trees nearby, a couple of them weeping willows, with branches drooping down to touch the ground. Chickens scratched busily in the dirt. At our approach, several baying hounds came loping out, scattering the chickens in all directions.

"It's quite picturesque."

"I'll introduce you to the Hiltons, then I'll take you to see the school."

He drew the car to a halt and got out. I opened my door, a little apprehensive about the dogs.

"Down, Blue," called the man on the porch in a deep, drawling voice. "Git down, Bouncer."

The dogs subsided and I got out and went around to join Mr. Hooper. The screen door of the cabin opened and a plump woman of about sixty came out, drying her hands on her apron. Her face was round and smooth and beaming. She came across the porch and down the three steps out into the yard to meet us.

"Hello, Clemmy," Mr. Hooper said affably, holding out his hand.

She took the hand and welcomed him in a soft, slow drawl, still beaming.

"I've brought the new schoolteacher to meet you."

She turned to me. I smiled and put out my hand, but she put her arms around me and enfolded me in a soft, warm embrace. I was startled, but hoped she didn't notice.

"My, my, ain't you purty?" she crooned, holding me at arm's length. "Not much more'n a child yerself. Come on in an' set down a spell."

"Thank you, Mrs. Hilton. My name is Anne Davis."

"That's a right purty name. Come in ta th' house."

We followed her up onto the porch. The man there hadn't moved but his keen eyes were studying me.

"Miss Davis, this is Willy Hilton."

"I'm glad to meet you, Mr. Hilton."

He didn't speak but gave a brief nod in my direction, his eyes still keen and unwavering on me.

"I'll just sit out here on the porch, Clemmy, while you get acquainted with Miss Davis," Mr. Hooper said. He drew up another old rocker and sat down. "Davy around?"

"He's in town, stayin' with John fer a spell."

Mr. Hooper nodded. "Maybe I'll look him up there, haven't seen him for awhile. You go on in, Miss Davis. I'll be wanting to go on to the school in a few minutes. Have to be back in town by four."

I followed Mrs. Hilton inside. What I saw there reassured me. The room was homespun but clean. There were two more rockers with plump pillow on seat and back. The sofa was covered with a beautiful patchwork quilt, rag rugs were scattered about the floor. A potbellied stove stood in one corner of the room.

"It's very kind of you to have me here, Mrs. Hilton," I said.

"Th' teacher always stays with us, ever since th' young-'uns was little an' we first started school out here. This here is your room."

She took me into the kitchen and pushed open a door along the east wall. I went inside and looked around while she waited in the doorway.

It was a simple room, but clean and comfortable-looking. There was a high bed covered with another patchwork quilt. Beside the bed was a desk with a kerosene lamp on it and a chair pushed under it. The rest of the furniture consisted of a huge wardrobe, a rocker with cushions, and near the door a small table holding a big enamel pitcher and a shallow enamel pan. A mirror hung on the wall above. This then was my bathing facility. My eyes lingered until I became aware that Mrs. Hilton was watching me with a certain amount of apprehension. I let my gaze drop to the rag rug on the floor.

"It's a beautiful room," I said honestly. "It looks very comfortable and homey. I'm sure I'll have everything I need here."

She beamed again. "My son Davy built th' desk an' wardrobe special for the teacher. That's his work."

"They're very nice."

"Will ya be comin' right soon then?"

"I'll come next Sunday afternoon since school starts the next day. Don't go to any trouble for me."

"Ain't no trouble," she said, patting my shoulder. "It'll be right nice havin' someone young an' purty around. I got a daughter 'bout your age. She's got four young'uns."

"Four?"

"Only one in school yit, a girl. It's good they found a teacher. Looked like we wasn't gonna have one fer awhile. Th' young'uns need schoolin'."

"How many grandchildren do you have?"

"Forty-some-odd, I reckon. Five great gran'kids."

"And do most of them live around here?"

" 'Bout half. We lose a lot of 'em to the city, my boys John an' Al an' three of th' girls. Been a right smart time since I seen some of 'em."

"I'm looking forward to meeting the grandchildren who will be my students. I suppose I should go now. I want to see the school and Mr. Hooper wants to get back to town."

She came out into the yard to see us off. Mr. Hilton stayed in his chair. I glanced back and saw him lean over and spit. Sure enough, there beside his chair was the bright red coffee can. I averted my eyes quickly and followed Mr. Hooper out to the car.

"Well, what do you think?" he asked me.

"I think it's going to be quite an experience."

"Get along with Clemmy?"

"She made me feel right at home."

"Good. The school is just over this hill. It's within walking distance, another reason why the teacher stays with the Hiltons. There'll be many times when it'll be too muddy or slick to drive."

When we stopped, I sat there a minute, looking at the scene. It was a typical one-room country schoolhouse, the yard fenced but badly overgrown with weeds. There were two outdoor toilets in the back with protective walls around them, separated by some twenty or so yards. In front was a long-handled pump located in the center of a bare patch. The schoolhouse itself was slightly in need of paint, with a small front porch, and tall windows on the south and east sides.

"Have to ask Davy to mow that yard this week for sure," Mr. Hooper observed. "Well, let's take a look inside."

He fitted a key into the padlock on the front door. He pushed open the door and stood back to let me precede him, reaching over my shoulder to switch on the light.

"Electricity, no less," he said.

"Why don't the Hiltons have electricity?"

"Don't want it, I understand, at least Willy doesn't. He doesn't believe in newfangled gadgets. Davy offered to have the cabin wired when he had the shop done, but Willy refused. A case of not missing what you've never had, I suppose. Actually, almost no one out here has electricity yet."

"All this in the enlightened nineteen-fifties too," I said, wandering around the room.

There were six rows of desks with seven desks in each row, starting with the larger desks against the south wall and each row getting smaller. Desks in the last row were small indeed, to accommodate first graders. In the northeast corner was a mammoth stove.

"Wood?" I asked, touching the cold metal.

"Yes, only economical kind of heat out here."

"Isn't it dangerous for the little ones to be so close?"

"There's an outside wall. Look."

He opened the furnace door and showed me. The outside was a wall encasing a huge stove with an air space of some twelve inches between.

"But the metal would still get hot, wouldn't it?"

"It's insulated, see?"

"Hm-m-m."

The north wall was bare. There was a rather unsteady looking ping-pong table pushed up against it. In the north-west corner was a door. I pushed it open.

"The cloak room," Mr. Hooper said.

There was a shelf along the top wall and hooks at regular intervals. Another door opened out onto the front porch.

"Where are all the books?"

"Here."

He indicated double doors at either side of the west wall. I opened one and it was a built-in bookcase filled with odds and ends of books. I looked into the other one and found it very much the same. The books were mostly old and rather shabby.

"We're going to need some more up-to-date books, Mr. Hooper."

"I'll see what I can do."

There was a large desk and chair facing the room, a long bench directly in front of the desk and a single blackboard on the wall behind the desk. I pulled the chair out and started to sit down. Mr. Hooper put out a hand to stop me.

"See that hollow in the seat of your chair?"

"Yes."

"Beware, Miss Davis. It holds a nice full glass of water. I've had experience."

I smiled. "Thanks for the warning. What other goodies are in store for me?"

"Maybe a wooly worm or a bug or a small grass snake in your desk drawer."

"Now you tell me."

"Harmless mischief. If you don't run into anything worse than that, you'll be fortunate."

"Are you trying to scare me off?"

"No, merely trying to prepare you a little."

"Thanks a lot. Do you have the key to this desk?"

He fished in his pocket and came up with a key. There

was very little in the drawer except for a long, flat ledger. I took it out and thumbed through it. It was last year's school record.

"Mind if I take this with me?" I asked.

"Go ahead. Seen enough?"

"I think so. This room needs a good cleaning, but I can do that next Sunday afternoon. What's on the floor?"

"Oil."

"Oil?"

"It helps keep the dust and dirt down."

"Also creates a mess. Ah well, when in Rome do as the Romans do."

"A good philosophy for out here, Miss Davis. Some of the people here are slow to accept change. Be careful about the reforming spirit. There's a lot needs to be done, I know, but it has to be done gradually. Stop, look and listen before you proceed, Miss Davis, and if you have any questions or problems, let me know."

"Thank you. I'll remember."

"Think you can find your way back out here next weekend?"

"Yes, I was careful to watch closely. Well, I'm ready."

I looked around the room again, then followed him out.

CHAPTER TWO

First Day of School

Monday morning I stood at the front of the schoolroom and watched my students arrive. True to Mr. Hooper's word, many of them were barefoot and dressed poorly. But most of them were clean. They came in all sizes and all ages, many of the older ones dragging little ones along by the hand. They were quiet and seemed very shy of me, stealing surreptitious glances up at me from lowered eyes.

At five minutes before nine I took up the long-handled bell on my desk, went out on the porch and rang it. I had to smile a little to myself, thinking of the very modern school in St. Louis where I had taught the previous two years.

The children who lingered out in the schoolyard now came in, among them three good-sized older boys. One of them was as big as a full-grown man, towering over my own five-feet-four by several inches. I felt a flicker of apprehension. At nine o'clock I rose and stood beside my desk.

"Hello, everyone," I said with what I hoped was a friendly, composed smile. "I'm Miss Davis. I'm glad to be with you this morning and I hope you'll bear with me until I learn all your names. As I call your name, will you please answer 'here' and raise your hand?"

I seated myself again behind the heavy desk and took up the long flat book. As I called their names I strove to fit the name to the child. Several of them answered to the name of Hilton, including the bigger boy. He was Luther Hilton and according to the record, he was fifteen years old and had failed seventh grade twice.

I deleted three names from the book (the Wilsons had moved away) and added four names, three girls and a boy who were starting first grade.

The rest of the morning was spent changing the seating arrangement according to grade, and passing out books and assignments.

At noon I took out the lunch Mrs. Hilton had packed for me—two biscuit sandwiches, one with egg and one with sausage, and a slice of spice cake. I ate at my desk, then went out to the pump to wash my hands and get a drink of water. The children were drifting about the schoolyard, slowly gathering into small groups or pairing off with heads bent close in confidential conversation.

The schoolyard had been mowed and cleaned up. There was a volleyball court and some of the older children had put the net up and were hitting the ball back and forth. There was a place fixed up for high jumping and broad jumping. It consisted of two wooden posts with large nails driven in on one side at two-inch intervals and a cane pole laid across the nails. A pit had been dug and filled with sawdust so the jumper wouldn't land on hard earth. That seemed to be the extent of the playground equipment. It wasn't enough. I'd have to see if we could get more, or organize some games or something.

I visited the girls' toilet, then returned to the classroom where I made an attempt to get acquainted with the shy little first graders.

At five minutes before one I went out and rang the bell again, which was the signal for a last minute dash to the toilet and to the pump for a drink, then back to the classroom.

The afternoon passed fairly smoothly and at four o'clock, I dismissed the children for the day.

"All right, children," I said. "School is over for today. Tomorrow we'll get down to regular classes. I've enjoyed meeting all of you and I'm looking forward to getting better acquainted. Please put your books away neatly in your desk, except, of course, the ones you'll want to take home with you. Pick up any papers that might be under your desk. Now I'd like for you to file out, one row at a time, please. The third row will go first."

I bade them goodbye as they filed past me. They all seemed cooperative. Of course, it was only the first day but I wanted to start as I intended to go on. I had always considered discipline and good order to be of first importance in the classroom.

With the last child gone, I went around straightening up the room, closing windows and picking up odds and ends of papers. Then I gathered up my own books, went out and padlocked the door and started the quarter mile walk back to the Hilton home.

It had not been a bad beginning, I thought, but it would be a real challenge. All those grades, all the different degrees of interest and intelligence, all the subjects that had to be taught. I had my work cut out for me, certainly, but I felt I was going to thoroughly enjoy it.

CHAPTER THREE

Davy

*T*he kitchen was stifling hot, even though I stood near an open window. Mrs. Hilton bent over the stove, turning the chicken she was frying. I watched her and had to admire her fortitude. That woodburning stove was giving out an overpowering blast of heat, her face was red and perspiring.

The air was filled with the redolent smell of the chicken and the inevitable corn bread baking in the oven. On the back of the stove was a large pot of green beans picked fresh from the garden that day and cooked with potatoes and onions and seasoned with bacon grease. An enormous black-berry cobbler sat cooling on a nearby counter.

It was a special meal. They must be having company again. Someone was always dropping in, a son or daughter, or a grandchild, or one or two of Mr. Hilton's cronies. Inevitably, they always seemed to appear at meal time. I had developed a real sympathy for Mrs. Hilton. She seemed to slave over that hot stove almost from morning until night.

She churned every day in a big stone churn and used the buttermilk to make soda biscuits such as I'd ever tasted before, large and light and fluffy. She made buttermilk pancakes and we ate them with butter or sorghum, or homemade jam or jelly. She used butter in place of shorten-ing and bacon grease for frying and seasoning. Every evening she baked a huge pan of corn bread and I wondered where it all went until I discovered Mr. Hilton used it to feed his hounds. She baked, she canned, she heated water for washing

14

dishes and for bathing and washing clothes. She never seemed to stop, while her husband sat gossiping with one or the other of his cronies under a shade tree, or went off hunting with his gun over his shoulder and his hounds at his heels.

"How many for supper?" I asked Mrs. Hilton now.

"Four. Davy's home for a spell."

Davy, the youngest son, the one Mr. Hooper said had so much influence with the children and would help me if I had any disciplinary problems. All this was for him then. As I took the heavy plates down and began to set the table, I wondered about Davy. I hoped I'd get along with him as well as I got along with his parents. Somehow, I was a little apprehensive about his arrival.

"Is there anything else I can do, Mrs. Hilton?" I asked, the table ready.

"You can go down to the crick and bring back a jug of milk if you've a mind to," the older woman answered in her mild, slow drawl. "Bring some butter too, I've about used this all. Oh, and on th' way back would you jist stop at the shop and tell the men supper is 'bout ready? Likely Dad will be there with Davy."

"Yes, I'll be glad to," I replied with perfect truth, glad of a reason to leave the overheated room. I closed the screen door carefully. Mrs. Hilton waged a constant warfare against flies with her flyswatter.

I started down the path toward the creek, breathing deeply of the cooler air. The dog Brownie came bounding up and went ahead of me down the path, making divergences to right and left, his nose to the ground, his tail swishing back and forth. He was a mongrel, the only dog the Hiltons had that wasn't a hound. He had made overtures of friendship to me right from the first. The hounds ignored me and gave me the impression that they thought I was an inferior person.

The air was noticeably cooler as I neared the creek. I could hear the rush of the swift water over the rock bed, could see the water sparkling in the sunlight. Mrs. Hilton said her children always swam and bathed in the creek in the summertime. It looked tempting to me today after the heat of the kitchen.

At the edge of the creek, I bent and let the cool water run over my hands and wrists, then cupped water in my hands and splashed it on my face. I dried on my full cotton skirt, then moved further down the creek to duck under the drooping branches of an overhanging weeping willow. I bent and lifted the heavy lid of a large wooden box that rested in the water. Inside were two gallon jugs of milk and a tall crock fitted with a cover. There were holes cut in the sides of the box to let the swift cold water flow through and around the jars.

I took a bowl of butter from the crock and one of the cold jars of milk and closed the lid. Out from under the drooping willow, I straightened and looked around with a sigh of pleasure. It was so beautiful and peaceful. I was glad to be here.

I started back to the house, aware of the small sound Brownie was making somewhere off the the right. Suddenly he came charging toward me, startling me into almost dropping the butter. He stopped dead in front of me, his hair raised up on his neck, a low growl in his throat. I looked ahead and saw a large brown snake coiled in the path. I gasped and took a step back.

Brownie stepped lightly off the path and circled around to the left. I called to him but he paid no attention. In a sudden flash he was upon the snake and had its neck between his teeth and was lashing it back and forth so rapidly that the snake was almost a blur in my vision.

I watched, my heart pounding, until Brownie dropped the snake and it lay there writhing and broken and bleeding. Brownie apparently wasn't satisfied though. He grabbed the snake and shook it again and this time the head went flying off and whizzed past me, so that I gave a wild little shriek of fear.

"All right, Brownie," I said, my voice shaky. "Good dog, good old Brownie." I shifted the butter and bent down to pat him when he came over to me, tongue lolling, tail wagging eagerly, an idiotic grin on his face. "Thank you. Am I glad you decided to come with me, you may have saved my life. I'll give you my share of corn bread tonight. Come on and stay with me, will you? Mrs. Hilton mentioned snakes, but I'd forgotten."

The dog ran on ahead of me, and I glanced warily to right and left as I went along the path. When I stepped into the bare dirt around the house I heaved a sigh of relief and wondered if it was because of snakes that they had no grass in the yard. I started on up to the house, then remembered that I was supposed to stop at the shop and call the men in to supper.

The shop was a well-built newer building in much better condition than the house was. The door was open but because of the glare of sunlight in my eyes, I couldn't see inside. Someone was whistling softly as I raised my hand and knocked. Immediately the whistling stopped.

"Yes?"

A tall young giant stood in the doorway. I raised my hand to shield my eyes.

"Mr. Hilton? I'm Anne Davis, the new teacher."

"Yes," he said again and I got the distinct impression of coolness, perhaps even of hostility.

"Your mother asked me to tell you supper is ready."

"Okay."

He turned back into the shop. I stood there a minute puzzled, then started back to the house.

"He doesn't like me," I thought. "He doesn't know me but he definitely doesn't like me. I wonder why?"

CHAPTER FOUR

Supper at the Hiltons

"There was a snake on the path," I told Mrs. Hilton. "Brownie killed it."

"I'm glad you had Brownie there. He's th' best snake dog we ever had."

"Are there many snakes around here?"

"We got three bad kinds, water moccasin, rattler, an' copperhead."

"This one was brownish with a design on its back."

"Copperhead, probably. They're worse than rattlers 'cause they don't warn you."

"I'll be afraid to leave the house."

"We don't worry 'bout them much. Ain't often you hear of anyone gettin' bit, but it's best to be careful an' stay on the path."

The screen door opened. Both Mrs. Hilton and I turned and saw Davy come in. I noted that he was quite good-looking in a rugged way. He was tall and wide in the shoulders, but otherwise slender. He moved with the feline grace I had noticed in others of these hill people. He went immediately to the washstand and began to dip water from the bucket into the wash pan. His mother poured hot water for him from the teakettle on the stove, then went back to taking up the chicken.

I poured milk into tall glasses, but under my lashes I watched him. He bent his head and sloshed water over his face, then straightened, dripping, and reached for the bar of

18

soap. He soaped his hands and arms and washed them thoroughly, then took up the pan, pushed open the screen, and tossed the water out into the yard. Only after he had replaced the pan on the washstand did he reach for the towel and dry himself.

I didn't realize I was staring until I met his cool disdainful eyes in the small mirror that hung above the washstand. I averted my eyes quickly.

The elder Mr. Hilton came in, his pipe inevitably clenched between his teeth. He pulled his chair out and sat down at the table. It seemed to me that he always removed his pipe with reluctance, as if it had grown there and it was an amputation to remove it. He laid it carefully now beside his plate. Mrs. Hilton put the food on the table, including the blackberry cobbler. We were just filling our plates when there was a commotion in the yard. Davy leaned back to look out the window.

"Looks like Brad an' his family are here," he said.

Chagrined, I looked at Mrs. Hilton. She had risen from her chair and was going toward the door. A minute later she was greeting her son and his family with every appearance of pleasure. Doesn't she ever get tired of it, I wondered?

Brad was the second youngest Hilton son and the father of that overgrown schoolboy, Luther. I saw, as the family came in, that he was also the father of two more of my students, two girls, ages about ten and twelve. I had known of course that they were Hiltons, but not that they were Luther's sisters. There were two other children, a boy of about five and a girl of about three. The little ones were barefoot and shy.

There were no introductions, but the parents both said "hi" to me and I said "hello" in return. I smiled at the children and got up to get more plates. Mrs. Hilton had already invited them to share the meal.

"Davy, go down and get three or four jars of peaches and

some bacon and chow-chow," Mrs. Hilton said.

She bustled about, poking up the fire and slapping the two iron skillets back on the stove. She took a big bowl of eggs and began breaking them into another bowl. I poured seven more glasses of milk while the family seated themselves. When Davy came back from the cellar, everyone was digging into the food. He put the things on the counter and rejoined them at the table. I resented them all on Mrs. Hilton's account. Some of them could at least have offered to help her.

"What can I do, Mrs. Hilton?" I asked quietly.

"Would you open them jars of peaches and put them in a big bowl? An' open the chow-chow too an' jist put it on th' table like it is."

I discovered when I opened it that chow-chow was a kind of homemade relish. I put the big bowl of home-canned peaches in the center of the table and Brad reached for the spoon before the bowl had properly left my hands.

"You'd think they were on the verge of starvation," I thought resentfully.

Later I was to learn I hadn't been far off. Brad had a habit of going into town on Saturday night after payday and coming home drunk and empty-handed. At those times the family descended on Mrs. Hilton for a proper feed.

Now the food on the table fast disappeared. Mrs. Hilton put the scrambled eggs and thick bacon before them and it vanished almost immediately. I had some of the green beans and potatoes and a piece of bacon. I didn't think Mrs. Hilton got even that much and probably she'd have to make another big pan of corn bread for the dogs too.

After the meal, the men leaned back in their chairs and talked dissolutely. Davy was pleasant, even indulgently affectionate toward the children and I could see that they were fond of him. He ignored me as if I didn't even exist, not once speaking to me or even looking at me.

I went about helping to clear the table as quietly as possible. Finally Brad and his father went into the living room. Davy invited Luther out to his shop with him, and the four younger children went outside to play. We three women were left in the hot kitchen to deal with a mountain of dirty dishes.

CHAPTER FIVE

Luther

*T*wo days later, I again stood before the open shop door and knocked. This time the sun was not in my eyes and I could see Davy Hilton sitting relaxed, whittling on a piece of wood. He looked up and when he saw me, he frowned. I didn't wait for an invitation but stepped inside and stood before him.

"I want to talk to you," I said almost rudely.

"I'm busy."

"I don't care. You've created a problem for me and I want you to clear it up. Since you came home I've been having trouble with some of my students. For the two weeks prior to that, I had no major disciplinary problems, just the usual small adjustments, but for the past two days, my classes have been repeatedly disrupted by the three older boys, particularly by Luther."

"What's that got to do with me?"

"Quite a lot, I think. When Luther's family came two evenings ago, Luther spent quite a lot of time out here with you. The very next morning he began the catcalls and the spitballs and the disrespectful gestures and it didn't take long for the other two older boys to join him. I hold you responsible for that, Mr. Hilton."

"I didn't say one word for or against you, Miss Davis."

"Excuse me if I don't believe you," I said, and had to make an effort to steady my voice before I could go on. "It's too much of a coincidence that it all started the very next day. It's quite obvious that you don't like me, but is it quite fair to turn my students against me?"

He was slashing at the piece of wood in his hand, his eyes lowered, and didn't answer me immediately.

"Well?" I demanded.

He tossed the wood and the knife on a table and rose and looked down at me, his eyes steel gray and steel hard.

"I wasn't aware that I'd turned anyone against you," he said.

"I think you are. What exactly do you have against me, Mr. Hilton?"

"I object to havin' a girl sent to do a man's job, for one thing."

"I'm not a girl, I'm twenty-four years old, and teaching is not necessarily a man's job. There are many more women teachers than men."

"That may be all right in town where there's a principal down the hall that you can call on in a case like this. Out here you're strictly on your own. It's ridiculous to think a girl as young and little as you are can handle them big, overgrown boys. I don't know what Mr. Hooper was thinkin' of."

"I was managing them fine until you came home."

" 'Cause they was lettin' you. You shoulda known it wouldn't last."

"And you feel sure you didn't contribute to this present situation?" I challenged him.

He turned back to his whittling and didn't answer.

"Can't answer that one, can you?"

I was aware that I was treading on dangerous ground, but I was so angry and upset I didn't care. I rushed on headlong.

"What business is it of yours, Davy Hilton? What right do you have to disrupt my classroom, undo all the good I was beginning to accomplish? Who do you think you are, anyhow?"

He turned on me, his eyes flashing.

"I'll tell you what business it is of mine. I've had it with misguided, helpless, female teachers. A girl, 'specially a city girl, has no business comin' out here, tryin' to teach this school. In the first place, she don't know what to expect. After her crusadin' spirit dies down, and th' novelty wears off, she starts to complain about th' inconvenience, th' loneliness. She expects to go into town ever' weekend and when winter comes that ain't possible. I'm tired of bein' nagged to drive women teachers into town, pullin' them out of th' ditch when they won't listen to reason, scoopin' snow for them 'cause they think they're too delicate to do it for theirself, buildin' th' fire for them 'cause they don't want to go out in th' cold, and makin' th' kids mind when they can't do it theirself."

"Have I asked you to do any of those things for me, Mr. Hilton?"

"You're askin' me now to make th' kids mind, ain't you?"

"I'm merely asking you to refrain from airing your grievance against me, or against women teachers in general, in front of my students. May I ask you to do that much for me, Mr. Hilton?"

"I told you I didn't."

"And I told you I don't believe you. If you didn't do it in words, you did it in attitude. You treated me like dirt under your feet that first night at supper, and Luther evidently noticed it. I don't think that was quite fair, do you? And by the way, I think you ought to know, Mr. Hooper didn't have much choice in hiring me. I was the only applicant for this school."

"It figgers."

"What does that mean exactly?"

"He wouldn't 've hired you if he'd had any choice."

"Perhaps not, but I'm a perfectly capable teacher, Mr. Hilton. I can help these kids get an education, given half a chance, and some of them want an education, excluding your nephew, Luther. It's not fair for one student to disrupt the whole school, and it's not fair of you to egg him on. And to think Mr. Hooper told me you'd be the one willing to help in case I had disciplinary problems."

"I told him last year I'd helped for th' last time. If he chose to hire another woman, I'd wash my hands of th' whole thing."

"Good. That suits me fine. All I ask is that you keep your nose out of my business, and let me get on with my job. Okay?"

His jaw was clamped shut, his eyes unwavering on mine, but he said nothing.

"You may not realize," I said, "that it isn't easy to pull up roots and come out here like this. Not many people can do it. If you succeed in driving me away, who will teach this school? You, perhaps? Was it you who drove Miss Smith away last year four months before the school year ended?"

I saw his arms flex as his hands clenched at his sides, and I was suddenly afraid. I backed toward the door, but gave him my last parting shot.

"I'm not so easily intimidated, Mr. Davy Hilton," I said. "From now on, you just mind your own business!"

CHAPTER SIX

Taking Sides

I was aware that I had handled that badly. If I'd waited until my anger cooled, if I'd appealed to him instead of challenging and bereting him, I might have accomplished a lot more. Instead, I had perhaps made myself a dangerous enemy.

I struggled through another day of school. Nothing had changed from the past two days. I was limp with exhaustion when the day ended, and nearly ready to admit defeat. Thank goodness, it was Friday. I'd go into town for the weekend and have a consultation with Mr. Hooper.

Unfortunately, Mr. Hooper had gone out of town and wasn't expected back until late Sunday evening. I spent a quiet weekend with longtime family friends, the Carters, did a lot of research on schoolroom discipline, then headed back to the hills Sunday evening.

Monday morning I found that all the textbook theories had no effect on Luther Hilton. He knew I couldn't do anything to him, he was much bigger than I. He grew worse as the day progressed and I was utterly undone. Schoolroom discipline and order had always been of first importance to me. Without it I was helpless. There was no point in trying to continue. I was licked and I knew it.

I walked back to the Hiltons' after school, feeling emotionally and physically drained and not a little bitter. I had failed after such high hopes, such confidence that I could cope.

Davy Hilton was sitting on the front porch, his chair tilted back against the wall. As I went up the steps I pushed the hair back from my face and looked him squarely in the eye.

"You win," I said dispiritedly. "I'll be leaving as soon as Mr. Hooper can find a replacement for me. If you happen to be going into town before the weekend, you might like to alert him."

I went on into the cabin, through the living room and the kitchen into my room and closed the door behind me. I was aware that Mrs. Hilton had looked at me oddly, but I was too weary and discouraged even to speak. I slumped down on the bed and sat there, staring at the wall.

Presently I sighed and got up. I should at least offer to help with supper, no point in sitting and brooding. I went back into the kitchen.

"Can I help?" I asked with an attempt at cheerfulness.

The faded blue eyes were looking anxious. I felt a rush of affection for her and put my arm across her plump shoulders, giving her a brief hug.

"Mrs. Hilton, I'll be leaving at the end of the week," I said. "But I want to thank you for being so good to me. I've loved being here and I'll never forget you and this place."

"You're leavin'?"

"Yes. I can't handle some of the older boys. At first things seemed to go along pretty well, but the last several days have been—pretty dreadful."

"Maybe you could ask Davy to help you. Sometimes th' teacher does. Seems some of the young'uns will listen to him when they won't heed their own folks."

I shook my head. Evidently she wasn't aware of Davy's hostility toward me and there was no point in telling her.

"He said, Davy said they need a man teacher here, and I suppose he's right."

"Ruthie says you're a right good teacher," the older

woman said with gentle distress. "She said all th' younger ones took to you right off, 'cause you make learnin' fun. Maybe if you jist talked to Davy."

"No, it isn't his responsibility. I'll talk to Mr. Hooper. Maybe there's a man teacher in the district who will be able to take over. I shouldn't have come. Mr. Hooper warned me there might be problems, but I thought—well, never mind. Shall I peel the potatoes?"

I didn't see Davy that evening, he didn't come in to supper, and I was glad.

It was after lunch the next day when I saw him again.

I was attempting to organize a softball game among the mid-grade children when, out of the corner of my eye, I saw Luther light up a cigarette. The other two older boys were standing with him and I knew it would only be a matter of minutes before he passed the cigarettes around. I sighed, not knowing what to do. Yesterday I had forbidden him to bring cigarettes on the school grounds again, and here he was openly defying me. Well, I would have to do something. I started toward him, and saw him snatch the cigarette from his mouth and drop it to the ground and put his foot on it. I was gratified but puzzled. Had something I said gotten through to him after all?

Then I saw the reason for his actions. Davy Hilton had straddled the wire fence and was walking toward them.

He greeted the three boys and stood talking with them for a few minutes, then he strode on over to where I was standing.

"Howdy, Miss Davis," he said pleasantly. "Tryin' to organize a game?"

I was surprised and it must have shown on my face.

"Why y-yes, I was," I stammered.

"You need a few more players. Hey, Luther. You too, Todd and Billy. Come on over here an' join us," he called.

They came reluctantly and he divided us up into two

groups, putting himself on the weaker team whose side I was on. He assigned us our positions and we started the game.

It was a rather inept game, but some of the kids seemed to be enjoying it, and the others didn't complain. Davy kept things going, calling out instructions and encouragement as if he really enjoyed it.

When I came up to bat he evidently didn't like the way I held the bat, for he came up behind me and instructed me on how to place my hands. I stood stiffly, imprisoned between his arms, and heard his hiss in my ear.

"Don't you dare pull away, an' try to look friendly, if that's possible."

I nodded, as if accepting his instructions. He stepped back, the ball was thrown, I swung and connected and the ball went into the outfield.

I flung the bat down and ran to first base, then on to second. Several small girls were scrambling for the ball. Davy was yelling for me to come on in, the rest of my team was jumping up and down and screaming. I made it in home before the ball was thrown, and Davy thumped me on the back so hard he almost knocked the breath out of me. I thought he did it on purpose but he was laughing down at me.

"See what you can do if you set your mind to it, teacher?" he said.

"Lunch period—is over," I panted, pushing the hair back from my hot face. "We'll have to finish the game another time. Ruth, will you ring the bell? And Mr. Hilton, thanks for playing with us."

I held out my hand and he took it. "I enjoyed it," he said. Then he turned to Luther who was standing nearby. "Want to go into town with me after school?" he asked.

"I guess so," Luther answered. "Sure, I'll go."

"Come on up to the house when you're ready."

"Okay."

He flipped a hand in farewell and the children headed for the pump for a drink and began drifting inside. Then he turned to me, his back to them.

"I hope that will help undo th' harm you say I've done," he said shortly, the friendliness gone. "I'll straighten Luther out, I gather he's your biggest problem. Mom wants you to stay, and in spite of what you think, I didn't deliberately try to turn Luther against you. I won't be givin' Mr. Hooper that message either."

He turned abruptly and strode away.

CHAPTER SEVEN

"Wood's Colt"

*T*here was some slight improvement in Luther's behavior that afternoon, but the next day there was a marked difference. I was intrigued and very relieved and wondered how his uncle had handled the situation. He was not belligerent as if he had been reprimanded, neither was he overly cooperative. He was there, indifferent and disinterested, but not disruptive. If he himself was not interested in an education, at least he wasn't actively trying to prevent the others from getting one, and where he led, the other two followed. Of those two, I felt the quieter boy, Todd Johnson, would soon be one of my better students. He had a keen mind and an active interest in science. His past grades went from excellent to failure, depending, I was sure, on where his interest lay. If he wasn't interested, he didn't bother.

That's where my responsibility came in. To me, teaching was not just an imparting of facts, but the ability to make facts challenging and interesting. I was determined to do just that. I would stay if Luther's behavior continued to be tolerable, but I was aware of a flatness in myself, a lack of animation that had always been a part of me. My anger against Davy was gone, but with it my original zeal and enthusiasm seemed to have gone too. It was going to be a real effort to keep my spirits up.

During supper that evening, I looked up once and caught

Davy's eyes on me. His eyes were keen, probing. I looked quickly away.

The Hiltons usually had no conversation at the table. They were there to eat. There was no lingering over food or pleasant conversation. When this meal ended, Mr. Hilton seemed to be in the mood to talk. He pushed himself away from the table and tilted his chair back, plying a toothpick in an idle, leisurely way. Davy did likewise. I rose and began helping Mrs. Hilton clear the table.

"Hear Jim's tearin' up jack 'round his place," Mr. Hilton said in his slow drawl, reaching out for his pipe. "Fixin' to build him a house like them city folks have, with runnin' water, 'lectricity, and don't know what all."

"Yep," answered Davy. "Got th' foundation dug a'ready. Wants me to help him."

"You goin' to?"

"Reckon so."

"What about John?"

"Buildin' seems to be slack in town right now. He's had to lay off a few men. Told him I'd take off for awhile and he can holler if he needs me."

"Jim gonna pay you?"

"Don't know."

"Reckon he'll have more luck keepin' that city woman of his'n happy in a fancy new house?"

"That's the idea, I guess."

"Shoulda had better sense than bring one of them city girls out here in th' first place. Shoulda knowed she wouldn't be satisfied with his ol' shack, but then Jim never did have no sense."

"Jim's okay."

I had to step over Davy's feet to get to the other side of the table. I might not have been there for all the notice he took.

"Oughta get started on a family, a kid ever' year, that'd

keep her busy," Mr. Hilton said, making a soft, puffing noise as he lit his pipe.

"Keep her pregnant and barefoot," I heard myself say drily.

"Eh? What's that you say?"

"It's something I heard before I came out here," I said, lifting my head and looking at him a bit defiantly. "The way you hill men keep your wives in subjection, keep them pregnant and barefoot."

It amused him. He gave a dry chuckle and winked at Davy. "Works pretty good, too," he said. "Th' little teacher here's got a lot of them citified idees too, but I hear tell she's a dang good teacher anyhow. How you gettin' 'long with that overgrown grandson of mine?"

My eyes went involuntarily to Davy and away again. "You mean Luther? I've had some trouble with him," I said.

"Oughta be out workin' 'stead of wastin' time in school."

"You think school is a waste of time?"

"For some I do. Never went to school a day of my life, but I get along."

"Times change, Mr. Hilton," I said mildly.

"Mebbe."

"While we're talking about school there's something I'd like to know," I said, my eyes going again briefly to Davy.

"You're stayin' then?" Mrs. Hilton interposed.

"Yes, I think so. What I wanted to ask is, who is the boy I've seen sometimes at recess hanging around outside the schoolyard? The boy who doesn't go to school and that nobody wants to talk about? He's about ten or eleven."

There was sudden, utter silence. I looked at the three faces, but none of them looked back at me. Mrs. Hilton was noticeably agitated. She made a helpless gesture with her hands and hurriedly went over to the stove and poured hot water from the teakettle into the dishpan.

"I'm not trying to pry into something that isn't my

business," I said slowly, "but it is my business because that boy should be in school. Who is he and where does he live so that I can go talk to his parents?"

The ensuing silence was broken only by Mrs. Hilton beginning to wash up. I frowned, puzzled. The front legs of Mr. Hilton's chair came down with a thump.

"Reckon I'd best get at th' milkin'," he said mildly. "You home for awhile, boy?"

"For awhile. I'll see to th' milkin'."

They both rose, Davy took up the milk bucket, and both of them went out. I stood looking after them a moment, then took a stack of plates over to Mrs. Hilton.

"Guess I've made a faux pas," I said almost to myself. "A boo-boo," I amended at her puzzled look. "Obviously the boy is taboo, but I don't understand it. If I'm not much mistaken he's a Hilton too. Won't you tell me, Mrs. Hilton?"

"Dad don't like th' boy to be spoke of in his house," she answered, her face hidden as she bent over the dishpan.

I sighed and took up the dish towel.

"All right," I said. "I'm sorry. Why don't you sit down, Mrs. Hilton, and let me do the dishes? From the look of all those jars, you've been canning green beans and beets all day. You must be exhausted."

"I am a mite tired but I'll wash up, then I think I'll go to bed."

"I wish I could be of more help to you. You work too hard."

After she went to bed, I sat at the kitchen table over my homework. Now that the weather was getting cooler, the kitchen was no longer intolerably hot in the evenings, and I had more room there to spread my books and papers out. I heard a sound outside and went to the window. Davy had his sleeves rolled up and was chopping wood near the woodpile. Mr. Hilton was disappearing over the hill, his gun over his shoulder, three of the hounds at his heels. I hesitated a moment before I made up my mind. I went outside and stood at a safe distance from the flying wood. He paused and looked over at me.

"Mr. Hilton, may I talk to you for a minute?" I asked.

"Again?"

"Yes, again. I'm not going to ask for any favors, just for a little information. Also I want to thank you for helping out with Luther."

"He's behavin' then?"

"Well enough. He isn't exactly cooperative, but at least he hasn't been disruptive since you—intervened."

"Does that rankle?" he asked with a small, sardonic grin, and I had to smile.

"You're very observant," I said.

"Wanted to handle it single-handed, huh? Come out here an' slay your dragons an' go back to th' city crowin'?"

"I suppose so."

"Are you gonna stay?"

"I'm going to give it all I've got. I have an uneasy feeling the truce with Luther may only be temporary."

"If you have any more trouble, let me know."

"I thought you'd washed your hands of helpless, misguided female teachers."

"I have more or less, but at least I can help keep Luther in line. It's—what Mom wants."

"Fair enough. What I wanted to ask you about is the boy I asked about at supper. Will you tell me who he is, please?"

"Not happy 'less you're stirrin' up trouble, huh?"

He bent and put another slab of wood on the stump he was using as a chopping block, and swung the axe in a mighty arch. The muscles in his upper arms and chest rippled, but he was breathing easy, as if he had not exerted the least bit of effort. I watched the powerful, rhythmic swing of the axe for some minutes before I spoke again.

"Your mother says your father doesn't want him mentioned in his house so I won't bring up the subject to them again, but we're not in the house now and you're a grown man and can speak for yourself, so I'm asking you to tell me."

He still didn't answer, busy throwing the freshly chopped wood onto the woodpile.

"At least tell me if he's ever been to school."

" 'Bout third grade, I think."

"Why didn't he continue?"

He shrugged.

"You know, but you don't want to tell me. You think I'm just being nosy, but I'm not. I'm here for all the children and that boy deserves the opportunity for an education as much as the others do. Who is he? Is he a Hilton? There's a strong family resemblance, you know. If you don't tell me, I'll keep on asking questions until someone does."

"Best let sleepin' dogs lie."

"I don't agree. What are you afraid of?"

"I ain't afraid of anything, teacher," he said a little mockingly.

"Then prove it. Tell me."

"Wood's colt."

"What's that?"

"Illegitimate."

"Oh. But surely that's no reason to exclude him from school."

"Up here we maybe feel a little stronger about such things than you do."

"So the son is to be punished for the sins of the father? You think that's fair?"

"Didn't say it was, did I?"

"But your parents are so kind and warmhearted. Surely—"

I stopped. Mrs. Hilton was kind and warmhearted, but was her husband? He was the one who seemed to be against the boy.

"Well," I continued, "you might just as well know I intend to do everything possible to get that boy back in school. I hope I don't step on anyone's toes, especially your parents', because they've been wonderful to me, but as teacher here, I have a responsibility toward the boy. What is his name and where does he live?"

"Name's Calvin. Lives 'bout a half mile north of th' school with his granny."

"How do I get there?"

"Have one of th' kids show you."

"Good idea. Thank you. I don't suppose you'd care to tell me why he quit school?"

"Didn't like it, maybe."

"Or maybe he was ostracized by the other children."

He didn't answer.

"Well, thanks for the information. I guess the rest is up to me. This is going to be quite a challenge. I hope I'm up to it."

I was almost talking to myself as I turned away, but he looked up, brows raised.

"Losin' a little of your aplomb, Miss Davis?" he asked drily.

"Where did you get your education, Mr. Hilton? From some helpless, misguided female teacher by any chance?" I returned sweetly.

"Nary a bit. Mr. Hooper is responsible for most of my education, such as it is."

"He taught here?"

"Yep, he taught here. Since then we ain't had a really good teacher out here."

"Thanks so much, Mr. Hilton. You are so kind and tactful. I wonder if I'll ever be able to like you."

"Don't bother."

"I won't," I snapped. "Unfortunately, as we have to live together for the next several months—"

"Live together, Miss Davis?" he interrupted sarcastically.

I felt myself blushing furiously. "Don't be funny," I snapped. "I meant in the same house."

"Not in th' same house. I only take my meals with my parents. When I'm here, I live in my shop."

"Did I drive you out, Mr. Hilton?"

"No one drove me out," he said shortly, a slight flush on his already ruddy face. "I choose to live in th' shop."

"I'm so relieved. Perhaps I can learn to tolerate you if I only have to see you at mealtime," I said sweetly. "Thanks for the information."

CHAPTER EIGHT

Snakebite

I had been going into town on weekends, but spending the time at the home of some longtime friends of my parents, the Carters. They made me more than welcome, and it gave me a chance for a long, soaking bath in a tub and an opportunity to do my laundry and ironing, and perhaps go out to a movie or a restaurant. It was a nice break for me and perhaps for the Hiltons too. I always went back to the cabin in the hills refreshed and ready to take up my challenging work again.

However, on the last week in September, it rained heavily on Friday and the roads were muddy and slick, so that I was unable to go into town. Saturday was bright and sunny and warm, so I decided to go ahead and do my week's laundry there. Mrs. Hilton took the washtub down from its nail on the inside wall of the side porch and put it on a bench. She put the washboard in the tub and brought homemade lye soap and water she had heated while she cooked breakfast, and I started on my laundry. I enjoyed the novelty of doing it in this primitive manner, but was glad there wasn't a lot of it. My knuckles were skinned raw by the time I had wrung the clothes out by hand and hung them out on the line to dry.

Davy and his father were away from the house. I didn't know where they were, but it was pleasant puttering around the house with only Mrs. Hilton there. After I finished my laundry, I cleaned my room thoroughly, then helped Mrs. Hilton clean the rest of the house. We had a cold lunch and my hostess spent a rare hour of leisure, rocking gently in her chair, telling me stories about her early days there in the hills.

We picked the last of the green beans in the garden and I helped snap them. Then Mrs. Hilton began supper while I brought in my laundry and attempted to iron a few skirts and blouses with her old-fashioned irons.

There were two of them and she put them on the hot stove to heat up, then showed me how to attach and detach the wooden handle. The trick was to take up one of the irons from the stove and iron madly until it cooled, then replace it on the stove and take up the other one. The irons were heavy and seemed always to be either too hot or not hot enough. I scorched a hole in one of my favorite blouses.

"Must be some ancient form of torture," I muttered. "Devised by a man, of course."

Mrs. Hilton smiled, she was relaxed and went about getting supper in a more leisurely manner than usual. I finished my ironing and put my clothes away.

"I forgot to get an onion when we was out in th' garden," she said, wiping her hands on her apron.

"I'll get it," I volunteered.

I went outside and Brownie ran over to me, tongue lolling, tail wagging. I bent and scratched behind his ears and patted his head. He and I had become friends and he often walked me to school in the mornings. Now he ran ahead of me to the garden and I gave a little skip out of sheer joy in the beauty of the day.

Suddenly Brownie gave a yelp of pain and jumped high into the air. I looked where he'd been and saw the long grass part in a slithering wave and knew he'd been bitten by a snake.

"Brownie," I cried in anguish. "Brownie, come here. Don't run. Brownie, don't run, please."

He was running wildly about, shaking his head from side

to side, rubbing the side of his face along the ground, all the time whining pitifully.

"Mrs. Hilton," I cried at the top of my voice. "Clemmy! Brownie's been bitten by a snake."

She came running out and between the two of us we tried to catch hold of Brownie, but he was hard to catch. When I finally did grab him, I saw that the side of his head was already beginning to swell. He must have been bitten on the jaw. He crowded close to me, whining pitifully. I couldn't help wondering if he was in excruciating pain, or whether he was afraid because he understood what was happening to him.

"What can we do?" I asked in anguish.

Mrs. Hilton shook her head in regret, stroking the dog's head.

"If I could just get him into town to the vet."

"Road's too bad and th' crick will be up. It'd be too late when we got there anyhow, more'n likely."

"We can't just let him die," I wailed. "If only Davy would come home."

Mrs. Hilton gave the dog a last pat and rose. I crouched there on the ground, holding onto him, trying to soothe him and keep him quiet, but he broke away from me and began running wildly about again. He disappeared down toward the creek.

"He'll be wantin' water. Poor ol' Brownie."

Tears were streaming down my face, she patted me on the shoulder. "There's nothin' you can do, child. Brownie's gettin' old, he's not as quick as he used to be, don't hear or smell as well, else he'd a smelled the snake even if he couldn't see him."

She went back inside. Brownie came back and came to me, pressing against my legs, whining. I bent and patted him, appalled at the amount of swelling around his head.

"Poor old Brownie," I whispered brokenly. "You're asking me to help you and I don't know how. I don't know what to do. At least I can get you some water."

I pumped fresh water into the dog's water dish and set it before him. He lowered his head and lapped at the water a couple of times, then went over and lay down under a shade tree. A minute later he was up again and back at the water dish, but he couldn't seem to drink. A rim of foam appeared around his mouth and he wretched violently.

For the next half hour he repeated this ritual over and over while his head continued to swell. I watched him and wept and tried to give him a little comfort. When I heard the tractor drive up to the barn, I fairly flew out there.

"Davy, come quick! Brownie's been bitten by a snake," I cried before he could even get down from the tractor.

I ran back with him right behind me. He knelt and looked at the dog and I knelt beside him.

"When did it happen?" he asked, his hand on the dog's head.

"About an hour ago."

"Did you see th' snake?"

"No, it was in the tall grass."

"Poor ol' Brownie," he said, reminiscent of his mother.

"Will you take him in to the vet? You could get through with the truck. I'll go along and hold him."

"It's too late."

"But you can't just let him die. You've got to try."

"He is goin' to die and there's nothin' I can do about it."

He got to his feet, looking down at the dog, his face remote. Then he turned toward the house.

"If it'd been one of your father's hounds, you wouldn't just let him die," I called after him, my voice thick and shaky.

I turned back to Brownie and saw my tears splash down on his head. When I looked up, Davy was coming back with his rifle under his arm.

"No!" I cried out.

"Go into th' house, Miss Davis," he ordered curtly.

"You can't just shoot him, you can't!"

"It's a long, painful death, Miss Davis. You don't want him to go on sufferin' for hours, do you?"

"He saved my life," I sobbed, rising and facing him. "If he hadn't run ahead of me the snake would've bitten me. Would you have just shot me too?"

"Go into th' house," he said again, his jaw clamped, his eyes like steel.

With a fresh sob, I ran toward the house. I had no sooner closed the door than I heard the report of the rifle. I went to Mrs. Hilton and sobbed against her shoulder.

"He had to do it," she said. "There was no other way. It was th' kind thing to do. It was hard for him. We've had Brownie since he was a pup."

"Was Brownie your dog, Mrs. Hilton?"

"No, he was Davy's dog."

"Davy's dog?"

"Yes. Gave to him by a friend."

"I didn't know that."

I went slowly into my bedroom. Through the window I saw Davy going down the hill, a spade over his shoulder, dragging a burlap bag behind him. I lay down on the bed and closed my eyes.

I didn't feel much like supper, but in a little while I got up and splashed water on my face. When I went into the kitchen, Mrs. Hilton was putting supper on the table.

"Where is Davy?" I asked.

"In th' livin' room."

He was sitting in one of the rockers, reading the newspaper. He glanced up at me, his eyes wary.

"I'm sorry," I said. "I shouldn't have said what I did. I had grown fond of Brownie and I—well, I didn't realize he was your dog. It must have been hard enough for you without—anyhow, I'm sorry."

He nodded but didn't speak. I turned back to the kitchen.

"Miss Davis," he said suddenly.

"Yes?"

"Stay on th' path when you go outside as long as th' weather stays warm."

"Yes, I will from now on."

CHAPTER NINE

Granny's Blackberry Wine

*O*ne of my older students, Ruth Hilton, or Ruthie as she was called, showed me to the home of Calvin's Grandmother Eldridge one Wednesday after school. I thanked her and she went on her way. I took my courage in hand and went alone up the path to the house.

It was an old house as most of them here seemed to be, and it leaned a little on the downhill side, but the surroundings looked neat and well-kept. There was a garden and the inevitable chickens pecking around in the dirt, but for a change, no dogs came running out to meet me. I knocked and a rather quavery woman's voice bade me come in. I pushed the door open and stuck my head in.

"Mrs. Eldridge?"

"Come on in," she repeated, and I went inside, closing the door carefully. The day was quite cool.

"Mrs. Eldridge, I'm Anne Davis, the schoolteacher," I said.

"I'm proud to meet you, Miz Davis," she said. She was an older woman, about seventy, enormously fat and indolent looking. She was sitting in a rocker, rocking gently, her glasses on the end of her nose, crochet hook and a doily in her hands. She beamed at me.

"Pull up a chair and set down," she commanded me.

I seated myself in a chair near hers and leaned forward to admire her handiwork.

"That's beautiful," I said truthfully. There were similar

45

doilies on the end tables and the huge chest that rested in one corner. The room was overcrowded but comfortable and clean.

"I'm makin' it for a gran'daughter of mine. She's gettin' married in a couple weeks' time."

"I'm sure she'll love it. Mrs. Eldridge, I came to talk to you about Calvin. I'd like to see him come back to school and I wondered if you'd help me."

She finished a few loops, seeming to concentrate completely on her work. I waited. Then she laid her work aside, and with a great effort, heaved herself up out of the chair. It creaked ominously. I thought she was going to show me to the door.

"You'll have a little glass of wine with me," she stated and waddled from the room. I heard her moving around in there and presently she came back with two glasses half filled with a dark liquid. She handed one to me.

"Thank you," I said, a little doubtful, looking down in the glass. It smelled good.

She lowered herself carefully into her chair and raised her glass to her lips. I took a cautious sip.

"It's very good," I said. It was. It tasted almost like juice, except that there was a mild tang to it. "Blackberry?"

"Yes, made it myself."

"Clemmy makes a lot of blackberry jelly, so I recognize the taste." I took another sip. "Mrs. Eldridge," I began again, but she interrupted me.

"How are you likin' it out here by now? Hear you're from St. Louis. Never been there myself, but I hear it's right big."

"It is. I like it here, though of course, it has been quite different for me."

"Clemmy an' Willy treatin' you right?"

"Of course. They've been wonderful to me."

"I hear tell Davy's back."

"Yes, though I don't see much of him. He lives in his

46

workshop, you know," I said, a bit defensively. I didn't care for the little knowing smile on her lips. "Mrs. Eldridge—"

"Most folks call me Granny."

"All right, Granny. About Calvin—"

Again she forestalled me.

"I heard about th' snake gettin' Brownie. That was a downright shame. I recollect once when Mr. Eldridge was still alive—"

She was off on a story about a mule of theirs that had been bitten. From there she went on to talk of other things. She told me stories about this family and that, and I couldn't stop her. I listened politely and from time to time tried to break in but she was oblivious.

I learned more about the people in the area in one hour with her than I had learned in five weeks with the Hiltons and my students. I had formed the intention of making the acquaintance of the parents of each of my students by visiting them in their homes, but after listening to her I began to wonder if anyone in the area was fit to associate with. I realized I'd have to try to forget everything she was telling me and keep an open mind and form my own opinions.

She refilled my glass and hers and as I sipped it, I found myself wondering about her and the kind of life Calvin lived with her. I guessed she was lonely and perhaps didn't have much company. I didn't believe she was malicious, but she certainly seemed to know all the shady things that had ever happened to anyone for miles around. I wondered how much of it she was making up.

I was feeling a little strange, lightheaded and confused and I had to go to the bathroom. Besides, it was getting close to suppertime and Clemmy would be wondering what had happened to me. I set my glass down and rose. I had to catch at the arm of my chair, appalled at how lightheaded and dizzy I was. Granny was looking up at me and her face wavered and swam before my eyes, her smile turning into a gloating smirk.

"Goin' so soon, Miz Davis?" she asked.

"I must. Clemmy will be expecting me. May I use your—" I hesitated before the word, I still had trouble using it, "your toilet before I go?"

She nodded and took up her needlework again. "Come again, Miz Davis. It's been right nice visitin' with you."

"Thank you," I said a bit faintly, wondering if I could make it to the door. "And thank you for the drink."

I made my careful way to the door, feeling as if I were moving in slow motion. Outside, I leaned against the door post for a minute and took a grip on myself. I looked around and located the outhouse some few yards from the house and made my way toward it, ashamed and chagrined that I actually swayed and stumbled a little.

When I came out of there I looked around to make sure there was no one around. Then I made my way slowly and unsteadily down the path to the edge of the woods. A little into the woods, I went around a wide tree and sank down gratefully at the base of it, not even thinking of snakes, only of closing my eyes and letting the waves of dizziness sweep over me.

I lay back against the tree, not daring to move, my eyes closed. Some time later a large rough hand was laid on my forehead. I opened my eyes and the face of Davy Hilton swam before me. I groaned and closed my eyes again.

"Oh, no," I said, "not you. Anyone but you."

"Been imbibin' a little too much, teacher?" he asked in a mocking voice. He slid one arm behind my back and the other arm under my knees and lifted me and rose to his feet. My head dropped against his shoulder, still swimming crazily.

"How did you know?"

"Granny Eldridge sent for me."

"Granny sent for you?"

"Yep."

"Then she knew. I had hoped—"

"You hoped she didn't notice, huh? No such luck. Are you sick or just dizzy?"

"Dizzy. I can't move."

"Relax, I'll carry you."

"No! No, just leave me here."

"It'll be gettin' dark soon. You can't stay here. A prowlin' bobcat might decide to have you for supper."

He carried me a short distance and put me down, propping me against a fallen log, keeping one arm around me as I slumped against him.

"Here, drink this."

He held a warm cup against my lips. I smelled coffee and took a sip. He made me drink more of it, then held a thick piece of bread to my lips. I turned my head away.

"I can't eat anything," I protested, half angry.

"Yes, you can. Take a bite, it's what you need. I'm experienced, you know. I got a brother who gets drunk ever' Saturday night."

Sudden tears smarted in my eyes. "I'm not drunk," I protested shakily.

"No? You hadn't oughta drink Granny Eldridge's blackberry wine on an empty stomach, you know."

"I didn't know. I don't drink and it didn't taste like wine, not much anyway. More like juice."

"An' you had a glassful?"

"Yes."

"Eat th' bread, Miss Davis. You need food in your stomach. You'll feel better in a little while."

Obediently I took a bite, then another. I lifted my eyes to his face and saw the amusement there. I felt my face pucker again and tears squeeze out the corners of my eyes.

"Don't cry," he said almost gently. "Granny's wine packs

quite a wallop even for an experienced drinker and I don't expect you're very experienced. You're not old enough."

"You're not angry?"

"Angry?"

"Because you had to come after me."

"No, I'm not angry. Eat th' rest of th' bread."

"You say she sent for you?"

"Yep. She even supplied th' bread an' coffee."

"I shall die of humiliation. How did she send for you?"

"She sent Calvin."

"Oh, I didn't see him."

"He keeps to hisself."

I was quiet, my eyes closed, still leaning against him. I was helpless to do otherwise, though I was feeling less dizzy.

"You're different," I heard myself murmur.

"Different?"

"You should be angry—"

He made no comment. I felt ready to doze off. He chose that moment to straighten me to a sitting position. I swayed and grabbed at his shirt.

"Any better?"

"A little."

"Drink th' rest of th' coffee."

I held the mug with both hands and drank it. When I handed it back I lifted my heavy eyes and looked at him.

"She tried to get me drunk, then sent for you and supplied me with bread and coffee. I don't understand. Why did she do it?"

"Granny's got a little bit of a twisted sense of humor. You're a young city girl, comin' here tryin' to tell her what to do. She'd maybe resent that a little, an' want to show you who's boss."

"More or less your own sentiments," I murmured. "I think I'll try to get up."

"Set still awhile."

I ignored him and struggled to rise. My stomach turned over and I subsided against the log, eyes closed.

"Satisfied? I told you I've had experience."

"I'm not drunk."

"No, just a bit lush."

"I suppose you'll tell everyone," I said bitterly.

"Tell you what, Miss Davis. I'll make a deal with you. I'll get you home without anyone else knowin', except maybe Mom, an' she won't talk. I'll keep my mouth shut an' I'll see that Granny does too."

"That might be a task beyond even you. You should have heard all the things she told me today."

"Granny's a big gossip, but she don't talk about th' things she does herself. I'll make sure she won't this time, and Calvin won't talk. In return, you'll agree to bury the hatchet."

I opened my eyes wide at that. "But you were the one—"

"I know, but there was reasons—but that's not th' point. I shouldn't've prejudged you. I'll admit, at least to a certain extent, that I've been wrong about you. I believe you really do have th' kids' best interest at heart and want to do right by them. Well, I have their welfare at heart too, believe it or not. So for th' sake of th' kids, I'm willin' to call off th' dogs, if you are."

"Okay. I'm glad. You've more influence around here than I'd realized, and I can't afford to be enemies with you. Thank you. That takes a load off my mind."

"Feelin' better?"

"Yes, I—think so."

"I'll help you up."

With his hands under my arms he lifted me easily to my feet. I closed my eyes and clutched at him again. He chuckled. My eyes flew open.

"Don't laugh," I said through gritted teeth.

"Sorry, teacher."

"Oh-h. I'm still so dizzy, everything is going around."

Before I knew what he was going to do, he swept me up in his arms and began striding off easily through the trees.

"If anyone sees—" I began.

"They won't. There's no one around except maybe Cal and he won't talk. Dad's gone."

"What about the cup?"

"Calvin will get it."

"Do you know him well?"

"Fairly well."

"His grandmother wouldn't talk about him, Granny Eldridge, I mean," I said relaxed and sleepy. "Would you help me there, with Calvin, to get him back in school?"

"Don't press your luck, teacher."

"He's your nephew too. You said for the sake of the kids."

He didn't answer. I closed my eyes again and relaxed against him.

"You promise you won't tell?" I asked anxiously as we neared the house and I felt the rumble of a chuckle against my cheek.

"Might make quite a story when th' men are sittin' 'round th' fire yarnin' on a winter night," he said.

"You promised."

"Okay, I won't tell."

Mrs. Hilton gave an exclamation of concérn as he carried me in.

"It's okay, Mom. She ain't hurt."

He carried me into my bedroom and set me on my feet. In a sweeping movement, he threw the covers back on my bed. I tumbled in and felt him remove my shoes and cover me. I pulled the quilt up over my head and heard him shut the door. I never heard the explanation he gave his mother, but she never once mentioned the incident to me.

CHAPTER TEN

Planning a Pie Supper

"**H**ow do you like living in a log cabin?" Mr. Hooper asked me the next time I went into town. I had gone to see him. It was the first time since I'd taken up my post as teacher in the hills.

"It's quite an experience," I answered. "I'm storing up all the details to tell my children and my grandchildren."

"Any problems?"

"Not at the moment, at least not any teaching problems."

"What kind of problems then, Miss Davis?"

"Those children, Mr. Hooper, are not on the same level of learning as most children of their age group. It's not their fault. Most of the books are old and out-of-date. We don't even have a complete set of encyclopedias. We need a new set of maps and a new blackboard, new and up-to-date science and arithmetic books, and I want some novels and magazines for the children and some new playground equipment — "

"Stop, Miss Davis!"

"Why?"

"Much as I'd like to supply you with all those things, I'm afraid the budget doesn't allow for it."

"You mean the children in my school, because they are poor and live way off in the hills aren't as deserving of up-to-date school supplies as the children here in town?"

"No, I don't mean that. I can supply you with some new books but the budget is limited, you know."

"Yes, I know," I sighed. "Give me what you can then, and if there are any old reading books tucked away somewhere that nobody is using, I'll take them too. I'm trying to develop a love of reading in my children and there are only a dozen or so books with stories. Oh, and if there are some songbooks too."

"I'll see what I can do."

"Thank you, and I'd better tell you I'm going to buy some puzzles and a few games and give them to the school. I'm also going to drive back to St. Louis this afternoon and gather up all the books I've collected over the years, all the books suitable for children, I mean, and bring them back. I'm not boasting. I'm just telling you so no one can accuse you of misappropriating school funds. Will it be all right if I stop back by tomorrow afternoon and pick up whatever you can supply?"

"About four? I'll make it a point to be here."

"Do you have a few more minutes? I'd like to talk to you about one of the children."

I told him about Calvin. He was aware of the situation and had himself talked to Granny Eldridge and she had agreed to send Calvin to school. Perhaps he'd gone, perhaps the other children made it difficult for him and he hadn't continued. One way or the other, he hadn't gone to school for two years now. Mr. Hooper was regretful but it was difficult to enforce the law so far out in the hills. The law required that all children go to school until the age of sixteen. Most of the children were through grade school at ages thirteen or fourteen, but there was no bus service out there to take them into town to high school, so most of them dropped out. Hence the difficulty in enforcing the law. If one child was made to go to school until sixteen, something would have to be done to the roads to make it possible for the rest of them to go on to high school. They were working on it, but progress was slow, discouragingly slow. There wasn't too much interest on either side.

He commended me for making an effort on Calvin's behalf and encouraged me to keep working on it. He asked about Luther, who would have been expelled last year if Davy hadn't intervened. I told him the story and he didn't seem too perturbed. He'd known Davy would keep Luther in line, he said. When I left, I felt he was quite satisfied with the way I was handling things.

I went back to the hills Sunday evening with my car pretty well loaded with books and inside games. Nevertheless, a lot more was needed before the supplies would really be adequate.

On Monday I spoke about it to Mrs. Hilton as I helped her prepare the evening meal.

"The children badly need new playground equipment. All they have is a volleyball, a lopsided softball and a taped-up broken bat. The trouble is, the school board doesn't seem to think the budget will allow for it, so I've been trying to think of a way we can earn some money ourselves. The children mentioned a pie supper. What exactly is a pie supper?"

"It's when folks have a get-together at th' school an' th' womenfolk bake a pie and bring it in a box. They decorate th' box up real pretty, and then they auction off th' pies to th' men, an' th' man gets to eat it with th' girl. They have contests too, like votin' on th' prettiest girl, who has th' biggest feet an' so on. All th' money goes to th' school."

"Does it bring in much?"

"Fifty, sixty dollars, I reckon."

"And do you have them here regularly?"

"Most ever' year. Not last year though."

"Then I think we'll have one this year and I wonder if next week would be too soon. I'd like to get the playground equipment soon so the children can get some use out of it before the weather turns cold."

"That'd be best for most folks. We don't get out much in th' winter."

"I wonder if you'd help me plan it, Clemmy? I've never been to a pie supper."

"I ain't been to one myself fer years. Davy there'd be more likely to know what to do than me."

I looked at Davy, tilted back in his chair reading a newspaper. He seemed to be engrossed in it.

"Perhaps the children will have some ideas," I said.

Nevertheless, as the evening wore on, I drew out more details from Clemmy. I took some notes. There would be a cake walk and Clemmy volunteered to bake a couple of cakes, a fishing pond where, for a dime a child was given an inexpensive toy on the end of a fishing line, a ring tossing contest with prizes, a prettiest girl contest, where the voters had to put up money to vote on a particular girl, the winner receiving a small gift. Also contests as to who had the biggest feet, the longest nose, the dirtiest ears and anything else anyone could think of. I became quite as excited about it as the children proved to be next day.

The date was set for the following Friday evening. The children and I found time each day to talk and make plans. I assigned three of the older girls to be in charge of the fishing pond, the cake walk, and the ring toss. When I went into town that weekend I bought balloons and crepe paper to decorate the school and spent considerable time picking out appropriate prizes for the contest winners. As a final purchase I bought a bushel of big red apples to pass out to the children after the pie supper.

CHAPTER ELEVEN

A Festive Air

*T*he big day dawned bright and sunny. The children bubbled with excitement and I finally gave up trying to calm their exuberance. We spent the afternoon cleaning the school building and yard and hanging the bright balloons and crepe paper. When I dismissed them for the day, gone was the orderliness I had been trying to drill into them, but this time it was for a happy reason. I merely laughed with them. It was evidently a very important occasion for them, and I had no inclination to put a damper on their excitement.

"Miss Davis, dare I believe my eyes?"

I whirled in surprise. "Why, Mr. Hooper! I wasn't expecting you."

"That's obvious," he retorted with dry humor.

I bit my lip, uncertain of his reaction.

"What's going on or shouldn't I ask? Why the festive air?"

"We're having a pie supper tonight," I explained in a little rush. "To raise money for playground equipment." An apprehensive pause as he looked around the room, then I asked, "Should I have asked your permission first?"

"Shouldn't you have?"

"I never even thought of it. Clemmy said they have one almost every year."

He continued to look around the room. His eyes went to the pictures I had hung on the walls, the small electric radio that I couldn't use at the cabin, the large vase of greenery on the small table, and lastly to the crepe paper and balloons hanging about the room. His eyes came back to me, he smiled, his eyes twinkling under the heavy white eyebrows. I sighed in relief.

"You've brightened up the room considerably, even without the balloons and paper," he said.

"You don't disapprove?"

"Why should I? I've never understood why some people feel a drab, bare room is more conducive to study. Quite the opposite, in fact."

"And the pie supper?"

"More power to you."

"Thank you," I said on a sigh. "I'm truly sorry I forgot to ask your permission, but it was all rather sudden, and we've been very busy making plans."

"What do you plan to buy with the profits?"

"The children have all kinds of ideas—a basketball and net, a new net and paddles and balls for the ping-pong table, a swing set, the old one is beyond repair. Then some jump ropes and indoor things, jacks, puzzles and such."

"Do you think you'll raise enough money for all that?"

"Probably not, but we can at least try."

"Good. How are things going otherwise?"

We talked for perhaps another half hour, then he walked back to the Hiltons with me, where he was invited to supper and accepted. The meal was more leisurely than usual with interesting conversation initiated by Mr. Hooper. He was evidently well known by them and there was a strong bond of friendship, especially between him and Davy. I was surprised as I listened to the two of them converse easily together. Davy's grammar was surprisingly quite good today, his conversation intelligent and well-informed. I couldn't help staring a few times. Evidently Mr. Hooper brought out the best in him.

After I helped clean up the dishes, I set about making my pie. It was going to be lemon meringue and just to be on the safe side, I'd make an apple too. I could cook but I wasn't used to a wood stove where the temperature couldn't be easily adjusted. Mr. Hooper and the Hiltons went into the living room, leaving the kitchen to me.

Already on the shelf there were three pies besides the two we'd eaten at supper. There was also a chocolate and a yellow cake that Mrs. Hilton had baked for the cake walk. They both looked delicious. I hoped my own efforts would be as successful.

Mr. Hooper soon took his leave, refusing the invitation to stay for the festivities. Clemmy came in and offered a few suggestions about the stove. Davy wandered in and took the milk bucket down and went to do the milking and other chores. I was just removing my pies from the oven when he came back in. They looked perfect. I heaved a sigh of relief and he grinned at me.

The rest of the evening flew by. I'd decorated three flat boxes the night before. Clemmy was sending along a couple of extra pies in case someone didn't have one. I went and dressed before putting the pies in the boxes. I put on a pale blue, full-skirted dress, much more dressy than I usually wore, and medium high heels. When I came out of my room the Hiltons had company.

It was their youngest daughter, Maggie, the one that was about my age and had four children. I'd met her before, her oldest daughter was one of my first graders. I now met her husband and the three youngest children. Maggie wanted to know if her mother had baked a pie for her, she hadn't had time herself. She was pretty but rather untidy, the children none too clean, the husband quiet and almost sullen. Clemmy brought out one of the pies and cut it and dished it out to the children. In an amazingly short time their hands and faces were covered with pie.

Maggie sat indolent, chatting with her mother. The children finished their pie and began wandering about the room. I was getting things together so I could drive over in plenty of time to get the last minute things arranged for the pie supper. There was a crash followed by an anguished wail. My lemon meringue pie was on the floor upside down and the four-year-old was clinging with sticky hands to his mother's skirt.

I looked at my pie and felt the prick of tears in my eyes. Maggie was scolding her son and he wailed afresh.

"Please," I said, "it was my fault. I shouldn't have left it so near the edge. He isn't hurt, is he?"

He wasn't and his mother pushed him away from her. He was ruining her dress. There was no apology for the ruined pie.

"I'll clean it up," I said, trying to keep my voice even. I had worked so hard on that pie and it had been perfect.

"Here's some rags, child," Clemmy said kindly. "You kin take one of the other pies. It's a shame, but no use cryin' over spilt milk. The apple pie is right nice too."

I cleaned industriously, my head down, fighting back my tears. I took a little longer than was strictly necessary, but when I rose, I believed I had my feelings under control. The first thing my eyes met were the eyes of Davy. He wasn't mocking me this time, his eyes were sympathetic, kind. I felt a fresh rush of tears and turned away.

"I'll carry that out for you," he said. I let him take the box I had filled with prizes and other things that might be needed. When he came back I was putting the pies into the decorated boxes, my apple pie and the two left from Clemmy's batch. I pushed one of them over to Maggie. Davy picked up the bushel of apples and took it out and I followed with the two pies. At the car he looked at me a little anxiously. I grinned at him. He looked startled.

"I'm not going to cry," I said.

"That's a relief. For awhile there I thought you was gonna be howlin' away with Timmy."

"I almost did. I put a lot of effort into that pie."

"Th' apple looked jist as good to me."

"I hope whoever buys it likes apple pie better than lemon meringue."

"It's th' box and th' girl that sells it, most times. Don't much matter what kind of pie it is."

"I thought no one was supposed to know which girl brought which pie."

He grinned again, looking down at my two gaily decorated boxes. "Sometimes th' guys get there early an' stand by th' door an' watch."

"Oh, yes, I suppose that's part of the fun."

"Is there more you want brought out?"

"Yes, the two cakes your mother baked for the cake walk."

We went back in together and brought out the cakes. I said good night to Clemmy as she was staying home and babysitting. Davy got into the car with me.

"I'll ride along an' unload th' apples for you," he said.

I drove carefully and he turned to keep an eye on the pies and cakes. After we unloaded everything, he stood looking around the schoolroom, his thumbs hooked in his pockets.

"It's changed since I went here," he said. "Teacher's changed too."

I was suddenly very busy straightening things on my desk. He was certainly different today, and I wasn't sure whether I liked it or not.

"Well, I'll be goin' if you don't need me for anything else."

I looked up. "No. Thank you for your help."

"See ya later."

With a flip of his hand he was gone. I went around making a last minute check on things.

CHAPTER TWELVE

Davy's Bid

*T*he schoolhouse was crowded and noisy. The fishing pond was almost empty. Several of the boys were occupied at tossing rings at a milk bottle. The crepe paper covered Ping-Pong table was piled high with brightly decorated boxes. I had asked Jim Baker to be master of ceremonies on the recommendation of the children. A sandy-haired, freckled young man with an engaging grin, he was standing behind my desk now, rapping for order.

"Now folks," he said when the room quieted, "first of all we're gonna start this here program off with a bang by havin' th' purtiest girl contest. Now you all know why we're here, to have a little fun an' at th' same time help our kids raise a little money for playground equipment. So open up them wallets, gents, an' let's have your nominations fer th' purtiest girl. Teacher here'll write th' names on th' chalk-board and how much you're willin' to spend on yer girl. All right now, let's hear from you fellas out there."

Names were shouted and dimes and quarters were brought forward. My hands flew at the blackboard, the dimes and quarters began to add up.

"Come on, gents, quarters an' dimes? That all ya got? Let's see a few dollar bills up here," Jim jeered.

"A dollar fer th' teacher," a masculine voice called, and flushing, I wrote my own name on the board and one dollar under it.

"You got real good taste, Ben. Anyone else wanna vote for th' little teacher?"

It seemed they did, several of my students contributing their dimes and quarters. It soon became a contest between two people only, myself and a rather buxom blond of about nineteen, who was smirking and chewing gum. I heard someone call her Goldie and the name was appropriate. Davy seemed to be the main one backing her.

"Folks, seems only fair for all of you to get a good look at th' two finalists, as they say in them telly-vision beauty contests. So how about if you, Tilly, come on up here an' do th' figgering, an' our two contestants come stand up front here. Miz Davis an' Miz Sutton."

There was clapping and stomping and whistles. I gave up my chalk reluctantly and came forward, my face felt hot. Miss Sutton rose from her seat and came to stand beside me, still chewing her gum, popping it from time to time.

The money kept coming in. My students, determined that I should win, went to their parents for more money, but every time I got ahead, Davy topped it for Miss Sutton. He was the only one backing her now. Sardonic amusement lit his eyes and twisted his lips.

At last there was silence. I was ahead by a quarter. Miss Sutton looked at Davy, her eyes pleading. He remained mute.

"Goin', goin', gone! Miss Davis is th' winner," cried Mr. Baker, pounding on the desk.

My students cheered. Flustered, I had to go get the gift I had chosen as prize for the prettiest girl contest, a gold-colored compact, and present it to Mr. Baker, who promptly gave it back to me.

"Now then, while th' purtiest girl has to stay standin' here with me—" His voice was drowned by hoots and laughter. His eyes snapping with humor, he tried to draw me close to him with an arm around my waist. I escaped and found a seat on the front row, my face burning, glad that my back was to most of the people. He had a delightful sense of humor, but I wished it had not been directed at me.

They went on to the contest for the biggest feet, which one of the Hilton men won, and I presented him with a huge pair of socks. For the man with the longest nose, I had knit a nose warmer. The man with the dirtiest ears got a bar of soap. It was all carried out in a spirit of good fun, no one was offended. The choice of Jim Baker as master of ceremonies had been a good one.

The pies were auctioned off and eaten. Brad Hilton bought mine and devoured half of it in a matter of minutes. Jim Baker bought Goldie Sutton's, and he sat there with her, clowning around while his wife sat with Davy, watching her husband with jealous eyes. Davy was talking to her, low-voiced, and at last she withdrew her eyes from her husband and seemed to be listening to him.

The crowd was quieter, their hunger satisfied, the room in wild disorder. I saw Jim and Davy in the corner, their heads together. When they parted, Davy sauntered over and took a seat. Jim went up and stood behind my desk again.

"Folks," he said, rapping for order. "There's one more contest that's been suggested, then th' cake walk, then we'll all go home."

"What contest?"

"A contest," drawled Jim and paused for effect, "a contest ta see who gets ta kiss th' purtiest girl!"

There was silence, then applause and calls from the men.

I sat rooted to my seat. My eyes went to Davy Hilton and he grinned mockingly. I glared at him.

"Come on, Miz Davis. Ya want to help th' kids earn all th' money they kin, don't ya?"

I rose reluctantly. It wasn't my idea of a joke. I'd get even with Davy Hilton for this. I turned and stood facing the audience and sent a withering look at Mr. Baker. He grinned back, unabashed.

"Jist look at her, fellas," he quipped. "Ain't she purty? Look at that curly brown hair an' them purty blue eyes, them sweet red lips. Seems to have spirit too, which adds a little spice. I wanna hear one of you fellas start off th' biddin' with a five dollar bill."

He got the five, then six. The bid quickly rose to ten and my heart began to thud sickeningly in my breast, for in the audience was a man who had repelled me from the start. He was unshaven and his clothes were dirty. He had ugly misshapen teeth, a weak chin, and the cruelest eyes I had ever seen. He was bidding steadily. The audience evidently shared my aversion, for they had quieted, become uneasy, glancing from me to him and back.

"Eleven," bid one of my valiant young students. I doubted he had that much money.

"Twelve," came back the reply from the undesirable character.

The bid rose to fifteen, then twenty and the bidders were dropping out. I tried not to show my fear, but my eyes went involuntarily to Davy. He had not taken part in the bidding, but his eyes met mine squarely, the humor gone. I swallowed and my eyes dropped to my hands, clasped in front of me.

"I have twenty-one, who'll go twenty-two?" No answer. "Come on fellas, look at her. This is th' chance of a lifetime." Jim was almost pleading, his banter gone.

Silence. I held my breath. The evil-looking one grinned. "Twenty-two."

It was Davy. A sigh went up from several throats.

"Twenty-three."

"Twenty-five."

"Twenty-six, damn you," was flung out savagely.

"Thirty."

The evil one ground his teeth. Jim didn't wait.

"Goin', goin', gone," he shouted. "To Davy Hilton."

There were cheers. The evil-looking man glared his hatred and he rose and left, followed by his companion. At once everyone became cheerful and rowdy again.

"Go on up an' kiss her, Davy," someone shouted.

"Make it a good 'un, Davy. You paid for it."

"Come on up an' claim your prize, Davy," Jim bantered.

He rose leisurely, sardonically grinning again and took his billfold from his hip pocket. He handed some bills to Jim and carefully replaced his billfold. I was nervous, irritated at the delay, though I was profoundly relieved that it would be Davy who would kiss me and not that awful man. He turned to me. I presented my cheek, but he took hold of my upper arms and bent and kissed me on the mouth, long and hard. I struggled, but he held me too tightly. I heard the guffaws and encouragement he was getting from some of the men and my anger boiled over. When he lifted his head and released me, I drew back my arm and slapped him hard across the cheek. The men roared.

"Kiss her again, Davy," someone called.

He stood looking down at me, his eyes flashed though he still smiled, a red mark appearing on the cheek I had slapped. I began to back away, he grabbed me and pulled me back to him and kissed me again. When he released me the second time, I would have hit him again, but he grabbed my arm and held it, laughing now.

"Let me go," I hissed through gritted teeth.

"I will, when you calm down," he said coolly.

"You—pig," I said.

He let me go and I fled to my seat and covered my face with my hands.

Jim announced the cake walk. I cooled off enough to shake hands with several of the people as they left afterward. I found I could smile again and speak quite normally. I asked one of my older students to pass out the apples while I spoke with two of the mothers who had questions about their children. I was able to smile and shake hands with Jim Baker and thank him for helping out. He was a little apologetic and inclined to linger. His wife came over and hooked her arm in his and pulled him away, giving me an unfriendly stare. My heart sank, wondering what all the women were thinking of me.

However, a few minutes later my most dominant emotion was fear. I was alone and it seemed as if unseen eyes were looking in at me from every window. I wanted to escape, to get to my car and back to the Hilton's, but I was afraid. That evil man might be waiting for me outside in the dark. Still, I couldn't stay here. There was no inside lock on the door and he might come in. I had to go, but I was more desperately afraid than I'd ever been in my life.

There was a sound, a movement. I whirled and saw Davy standing there. My knees buckled. I sat down hard in a nearby seat.

"Oh, Davy," I gasped out. "I was afraid. I thought—"

"Thought what?"

"I was afraid you'd gone."

"Thought you might need some help cleanin' up here."

I rose suddenly and snatched up my purse. "It can wait. Let's go home."

"Sure you want to leave this mess?"

"Yes. I'll—clean it up tomorrow."

"Don't you want to take th' money box?"

"Oh, yes, of course."

I took the money box and started for the door. There I hesitated, fumbling in my purse for the padlock.

He took it from me and locked the door. Then he took my arm.

"Don't be scared. I'll take care of you," he said and I drew a deep, shaking breath and relaxed a little.

"Slide over, I'll drive," he said, and gratefully I handed over the keys.

Once we were moving I relaxed still more.

"Thank you for coming back," I said.

"I never left."

"Oh, I thought—who was that awful man?"

"Name's Ned Reynolds."

I shuddered. "If he'd kissed me, I'd have died."

"No. More'n likely you'd have jist knocked his teeth down his throat," he said with wry humor.

I moved over against the door, becoming icily stiff. He chuckled.

"Remembered you're mad at me, huh?"

"I am furious with you. Your behavior was—was despicable."

"Why? Mighty expensive kiss if you ask me. Mighty expensive even for two kisses."

"It was your idea in the first place, don't try to deny it. I saw you over in the corner with Jim Baker."

"Jist tryin' to help. You wanted to raise all th' money you could, didn't you?"

"Not that way. That was the most humiliating experience I've had in my life."

"What? Bein' kissed by me?"

"Yes, and putting such thoughts in that awful man's mind."

"I'm sorry about that. Never dreamed Ned would take part in th' biddin'!"

"So you admit it was your idea?"

"I rescued you, didn't I? And you got thirty dollars more for your fund."

"I was just beginning to win the respect of the children and now they'll be laughing at me behind my back."

"You're takin' it too serious. Nobody'll think twice about it. It was jist part of th' fun."

"Fun! Is that why everyone was sniggering at me? A teacher has to have the respect of student and parent alike. I might as well resign."

"It'll all be forgot in a week or two."

"Easy for you to say."

We were silent the rest of the way. When he stopped before the cabin, I fumbled for the door handle, but he reached over and caught my arm.

"Let me go."

"No, not 'til you've calmed down. My sister an' her family are probably still there."

I slumped dejectedly and he released me.

"I'm sorry. It got outa hand. I didn't mean to start anything unpleasant. It was jist a joke."

"Some joke."

"Look, it will be forgot if you don't make too much of it. If you treat it as unimportant, ever' one else will too, you'll see."

I was silent, unwilling to help him.

"As for Ned, he won't bother you. He hardly ever comes around an' if he does, it'll be me he's after, not you. He don't like me much."

"Can you guarantee that?"

"He don't like women, stays away from 'em, that's why tonight, I never thought—you'll be safe. He won't bother you."

"I'm glad to hear it," I said sarcastically.

"Feelin' better?"

"I'm all right."

"Maybe you better go in now. They'll be wonderin'."

"What's the difference? I'll be the talk of the whole country by tomorrow anyhow," I said grumpily and got out of the car.

CHAPTER THIRTEEN

Ruffled Feathers

I was sitting over some test papers at my desk. The children had all gone home and I was alone. The outside door opened and a rather dilapidated old hat landed on the floor beside my desk. I gave a start and looked around. Davy Hilton stuck his head in.

"Is it safe to come in?" he asked humbly.

I lifted my chin but couldn't help smiling. He heaved a sigh of relief and came on in. He retrieved his hat from the floor, eyeing me with mock apprehension as he sat down on the long bench in front of me.

"Well, teacher?" he inquired.

"Well?"

"Still mad?"

"Haven't I reason to be?"

"Don't see why. Figgered I was doin' you a favor, helpin' you raise money for th' school."

"I'm not arguing with your motive, if that was your motive. It was your method I didn't approve of."

"How else could I have done it?" he asked plaintively.

"Never mind that."

"Are you still mad? I've stayed away four days so's you'd not be offended by my presence."

"Noble of you," I said, my voice dry. I rose to put papers in my desk drawer. He came to stand beside the desk.

"You didn't answer my question."

"Oh, all right. I'm not mad, not much anyway. I realize it was my own fault."

He blinked. "It was?"

"Yes. If I hadn't—I shouldn't have slapped you. You'd paid for the kiss, after all."

"That's what I don't understand. Why did you slap me? A few minutes before, you'd practically begged me to kiss you."

"I did not!"

"Don't fib, teacher. You know you did."

"I did not. I mean, I wasn't asking you to kiss me. I just wanted you to save me from that awful man."

"Well, it's th' same thing."

"I suppose so, but you didn't have to—oh, shut up, will you?"

"Why, teacher!"

I turned on him. "What's the matter with you?" I demanded. "Have you been drinking?"

"No. Have you?"

I felt myself flush. "You had to say that, I suppose."

"Sorry. Seen anything of Ned?"

"No, thank goodness."

"Didn't think you would. How have things been otherwise since I been gone? Any problems?"

"Nothing that I couldn't handle myself," I answered stiffly.

"Okay, teacher, didn't mean to ruffle your feathers. Mind if I ask how much money you took in at th' pie supper?"

"One hundred ten dollars."

"Whew, quite a haul. Jist think, without my thirty, you'd only had eighty."

"We could have managed with eighty, Mr. Hilton."

"So we're back to Mr. Hilton, are we? When I came back after th' pie supper, it was Davy, remember?"

"What do you want, Mr. Hilton? I'm busy," I said frigidly.

"I came to see how you are, if you had any problems I could help with, an' to offer to drive you into town this weekend in th' truck to bring back th' playground equipment. Also I was under th' impression we was gonna try to be friends."

I looked up. I had the strange impression I had hurt him.

"I'm sorry. I just—you seem different today. I didn't know if you were making fun of me, or just teasing me."

He relaxed visibly. "Maybe I'm the one should apologize. Been with Jim four days. His clownin' around seems to rub off."

"Oh. That would explain it. How is he?" I saw the look on his face and added hastily, "His wife too, of course."

He eyed me for a minute before he answered. "He's fine. They're fine."

"How is the house coming along?"

"Good. They'll be able to move into it 'fore too many months."

"I'm glad. Did I hear you offer to bring the playground equipment back in your truck?"

"You did, 'less you'd rather Jim did it."

"Jim? What do you mean? Is he going into town this weekend?"

"Don't know, thought maybe you did."

"You're talking in riddles. I'm afraid you'll have to explain yourself."

He sat on the edge of my desk, twirling his hat around, his eyes steady on mine.

"Jim mentioned you several times this week. Seemed quite taken with you. His wife didn't appreciate it too much."

"You're imagining things."

"No, but maybe she is. I told her there was nothin' to it, but she's jealous an' possessive where Jim's concerned."

"What does that have to do with me?"

"Jist thought I'd mention it. You seemed to like Jim."

"I did like him. Is there anything wrong with that?"

"I wouldn't advise you to advertise it. Sally's awful jealous."

"She has no reason to be jealous of me."

"You're pretty an' cute. Jim said so several times. It wasn't very smart. I'm jist warnin' you to be careful."

"You may inform your friends that I have a young man waiting for me in St. Louis," I said coolly. "I'm not the least bit interested in your Jim Baker or anyone else out here."

Davy got up. "Did you want me to drive you into town Saturday then?"

"If it's not too much trouble."

"It's not too much trouble. You ready to go now? Mind if I walk along with you?"

"Yes, I'm ready and no, I don't mind."

On the way home, he told me about Jim's modern house. He seemed quite impressed with it.

CHAPTER FOURTEEN

Friendship or Truce?

On Saturday I rode into town with Davy in his big truck and we spent the morning shopping. I had expected him to drop me off and come back later to pick up the things I bought, but he stayed with me. He hadn't anything else to do, he said, except pick up a few groceries for his mom, so he'd just tag along.

By noon we had everything and were back in the truck with me sitting in the middle of the seat near him. He'd put a box of groceries on my side by the door.

"I'm starved," he said. "Let's stop at th' next drive-in an' have a hamburger, okay?"

"Okay."

We both ordered cheeseburgers, French fries and strawberry malts. I reached in my purse to pay for my own, but he disregarded the bills I held out and paid for it himself.

"Thank you," I said.

"You're welcome," he returned, peeling the paper back from his sandwich. "Amazin' what a hundred an' ten dollars'll buy, ain't it?" he observed thoughtfully.

I looked up and met his eyes smiling humorously down at me, and I felt myself flush.

"There were some good buys," I said defensively. "Your idea of stopping at the used bookstore first was a good one."

"Um-huh. How much was it there? Only twenty dollars or so, wasn't it?"

I didn't answer, my head bent over my malt.

"Then only 'bout twenty at th' dime store for th' jump ropes, an' jacks, an' puzzles, an' games, but th' really great buy was th' swing set for ninety-seven dollars, don't ya think?"

"It had to be big and sturdy, one of those small ones wouldn't last a month."

"Right. Th' little ones will love it as much as th' older ones'll like the basketball an' net, an' the ball an' bats an' gloves."

He looked at me, eating his cheeseburger, eyebrows raised.

"Hope you're not expectin' to get rich this year, teacher," he teased.

I lifted my chin and tossed my hair back. "Yes, I am. Rich in experience and rich in friendship. Those things are more valuable than money, anyhow."

"Right."

"Besides, you paid for the baseball equipment."

"Couldn't help myself. Th' way you was lookin' at them gloves an' things, like a little kid with his nose pressed against a toy shop winder—"

"Don't say 'winder,' say 'window.' Your grammar and pronunciation are atrocious, and you know better."

"Tryin' to change th' subject?"

I ignored him and finished my lunch. He was already finished and was watching me, grinning sardonically.

"Stop staring, will you?"

"Can't help it, teacher. You're awful cute when you're mad."

"I'm not mad."

"Musta been my imagination, huh?"

He honked for the girl to come and get the tray, then started the truck. I sat back and tried to relax. In a little while I began to smile. I folded my hands primly in my lap.

"Speaking of friendships," I said demurely, "I've certainly

appreciated yours. Perhaps friendship isn't the right word, perhaps tolerance would be better, but—"

"Friendship will do."

"All right, friendship then. As I was saying, I certainly do appreciate it. My way has been made incredibly smoother since you've called off your dogs, to use your expression. Your goodwill means a lot, evidently, to judge by the attitude of some of your nieces and nephews."

"Since th' teacher always stays with my folks, an' I still live at home, I've been called on to help out in one way an' another. Th' kids have come to expect it, I reckon."

"So I gathered. Some of them have a tendency to talk quite a lot about their Uncle Davy."

His glance was wary. "What're you gettin' at?"

"Nothing, nothing at all. Only, as I said, I appreciate your help and your cooperation and mean to cultivate your friendship, but I'll try very hard not to take advantage of you too often. Also, I promise not to pull a Gloria Smith on you."

His face flushed darkly, his lips straightened to a grim line, his eyes looked straight ahead.

"Which one of them told you about that?" he asked.

"None of them. Actually, Granny Eldridge told me. I was glad to know the reason why you were so against women teachers, and that it wasn't anything I'd done personally. Very understandable, I'm sure."

"You're something of a brat, ain't you?"

"Possibly, but not, I assure you, a femme fatale."

"Neither was she, jist man-hungry, and at least ten years older than me."

"Poor Davy." I gave a little gurgle of laughter.

He changed to second gear to negotiate a sharp turn, his face still grim. "It wasn't a bit funny," he said shortly.

"I'm sorry. No, I can imagine it was excessively awkward and to be driven out of your own home to take up living in your shop—she must have been persistent."

"She was, an' if you keep talkin' about it, I'm gonna dump you out in th' road an' let you walk home, an' that's no joke."

"Sorry," I said meekly. "But I was relieved to know why you disliked me so much when I first came here."

"I didn't dislike you. Let's say I was a little bit—"

He stopped, evidently unable to find the word that would describe his feelings.

"Worried? Wary?" I suggested. "I assure you, I'm no danger to you. I value your friendship for what it's worth, but I do have that young man waiting for me at home, you know."

"Whadda you mean, you value my friendship for what it's worth?"

"To be on good terms with the top man in the area is worth quite a lot, you know."

"Thanks," he said drily, and I gurgled with laughter again.

"Friendship just for the sake of friendship is worth quite a lot too. I didn't mean I was going to cultivate your friendship just so I could use you."

"Sounded mighty like it."

"I was teasing. Pax?"

"You're a brat," he said again. "A spoiled brat, too pretty for your own good too."

"Thank you," I said demurely.

"That wasn't necessarily a compliment."

"I choose to take it as such. Are some of the boys going to be at school to help unload?"

"Luther an' Todd an' a couple of th' fathers, but before we change th' subject, if we're gonna be friends, th' subject of Gloria Smith is closed."

"Yes, sir."

"I mean it."

"Yes, sir."

"Thank th' Lord, we're almost home. Thought we'd never get here."

I laughed again but his look made my face sober and very solemn.

"Had your revenge now, teacher?" he asked softly as we pulled up in the schoolyard. He grinned at me as he got out of the truck and helped me down.

Luther was there with his father, also Todd and Jim Baker. Jim seemed unusually subdued and it made me feel uneasy. He spoke to me briefly and then they set about unloading the truck. Davy carried the boxes of books and indoor games inside for me and I began unpacking and putting them away.

Presently I looked out the window to see what progress they were making. Already the swings were up and they seemed to be contemplating where to put the basketball goal. I'd specified that it absolutely not be set up against the schoolhouse. About to turn back, I caught a glimpse of a small boy half hidden behind the fence. I felt sure it was Calvin and quickly went outside. He was so engrossed in watching he didn't see me until I was right beside him.

"Don't go, Calvin," I said quietly. "I won't hurt you. I'd like to be friends."

I stood a short distance away from him and kept my hands down by my side. I didn't want to frighten him, he was like a wild thing, easily startled into flight. I'd seen him hang around outside the schoolyard fence, then flee like a deer when anyone drew near.

"We've got some new playground equipment," I continued on. "Do you like to swing, Calvin?"

No answer, but he was looking steadily up at me, still in a crouching position.

"I love to swing. I used to spend hours swinging and singing when I was a little girl," I said. "Would you like to try the swings with me, Calvin? We'll be the very first to use them."

I put out my hand, he looked at it, then back at me. Slowly he rose and put his hand in mine. We began walking toward the gate, then toward the swings. He stayed close to me as if he might be afraid of the reactions of the men. I kept talking.

"I've been wanting to meet you, Calvin. I'm glad I've finally had the opportunity. Isn't it a beautiful day? Just right for swinging. Which one will you have? Shall I take this one and you take that one?"

He let go of my hand and climbed up onto one of the swings, pushing himself back with his feet. I sat down in the swing beside him and did likewise. We were silent, pumping ourselves higher and higher. His small face was sober and intent.

"Bet I can go higher than you can," I called, laughing.

His face broke out in a beautiful grin that was quickly banished as he put more effort into his upward sweep.

"Hey, you two!"

It was Davy. He was walking toward us, hammer in hand.

"Stop a minute, will you? I wanna make sure everything is tight before you go sailin' off into th' blue never to be seen again."

We slowed and stopped, and watching Calvin's face I saw that he was not afraid of his Uncle Davy.

"How you doin', Cal? Let me check your swing a minute, then you can show her who's champeen swinger in these parts," Davy said in an easy conversational tone.

He checked both the swings we were using, the seat and the upper attachment, then did the same with the other two. When he was satisfied, he stepped back and grinned at Calvin. "Go to it, young fella," he said.

I deliberately got off to a slow start. Calvin was swinging high into the air before I was swinging freely again. We must have stayed on those swings a good ten minutes before I began to let my swing slow to a stop. My legs and arms were screaming in protest. I hadn't swung like that for years.

Calvin continued to swing. I sat and swayed gently to and

fro and watched him. When he finally slowed to a stop, I grinned at him.

"You win," I said. "You're a better swinger than I am."

I stood up and he came down out of his swing.

"Would you like to come inside with me, Calvin? We got some new books and puzzles and indoor games today. I was just putting them away when I saw you. Would you like to help? Or if you'd rather play with some of the things or just look around, I'd be glad to have company."

I held out my hand again and he took it and went with me. He was fascinated by the books and spent some time taking them up one by one and turning the pages. I busied myself putting things away, but covertly, I watched him.

"Do you like to read, Calvin?" He nodded but didn't look up. I went over and knelt beside him. "What kind of book do you like best? About animals, about horses and dogs? We have all different kinds here. There's one about trains and even one about bridges. Why don't you pick one out and you can take it home with you and read it. Then when you finish it, you can bring it back and get another one. Would you like that?"

He looked up at me then, his eyes big and serious, and nodded again.

"Good. Pick out any one you want then and maybe you'd like to take a puzzle home too. We have several here."

He took quite a time over the selection of the book and finally chose Black Beauty. I thought perhaps it was a little old for him, but I didn't say so. I handed him one of the boxed puzzles.

"Will you come to school with the rest of us, Calvin?" I asked as he turned to go. "We have a lot of fun and we'd love to have you. We've been reading part of a story every day after lunch and we sing songs every morning. We work but we play too, and I think you'd enjoy it. Will you come, Calvin?"

He didn't answer, in fact, he hadn't spoken a word the whole time, but I felt he was considering what I said. He left then and I sat down in my chair and gazed unseeing at the door, my chin in my hands.

"Well?"

It was Davy standing in the doorway, and all of a sudden my eyes were filled with tears. I put up a hand to wipe them away.

"He took a book and a puzzle," I said in a shaky voice. "He's going to bring them back when he's finished and get more. He didn't say anything, but I think maybe he'll start coming to school. He was fascinated by the books."

Davy walked over and put his big, heavy hand on my head.

"Good girl," he said.

CHAPTER FIFTEEN

Jim Baker's Confession

I had gotten into the habit of staying awhile after school to straighten up and grade a few papers. The schoolroom was quiet. I bent over my desk, absorbed in my work until a sound at the door made me look up. Jim Baker was standing there looking at me.

"Hello," I said, surprised.

"Busy?" he asked.

"Just grading a few papers. I do sometimes, it's easier than carrying them all home. You wanted to see me?"

"Yes, I did."

He came on into the room, hat in hand. He was quiet, subdued, not at all like the exuberant young man I had met at the pie supper. I felt slightly apprehensive.

"About one of my students?" I asked.

"No."

"Then maybe we should walk on up to the Hilton's," I suggested, rising.

"No, please," he said earnestly. "There's no one around, they're all gone, I made sure before I came in." He drew a deep breath. "I wanted to talk to you alone."

I gathered up my papers and stacked them, eyes downcast. Davy's warning came back to me. I wished someone would come, anyone, and at the same time hoped devoutly no one would.

"Me an' Sally are havin' trouble," he said bluntly.

"Sally is your wife?"

He nodded.

"I never did really meet her, you know. I'm sorry you're having trouble, but I don't see how I can help you, Mr. Baker," I said formally.

"She's jealous of you. She's jealous of anyone I look at more'n once."

"Perhaps that's to be expected of a new wife. You haven't been married too long, have you?"

"It seems like forever."

"This really isn't any of my business, you know."

"Yes, it is, 'cause—" he stopped, flushing and turned his hat around and around by its brim. "She thinks I'm in love with you," he said.

"Why would she think a thing like that?"

"Look, mind if I sit down?"

"If you like, but I can tell you, Mr. Baker, I'm not very happy about this. I can't afford to get mixed up in anything unsavory. A teacher has to be very careful of her reputation. Something like this could ruin me."

He sat down, his head bowed, the hat still turning in his hands.

"Why does she think you're in love with me?" I asked.

"She's jealous an' suspicious of anyone I talk to or even look at."

"Is there perhaps a little more to it than that?"

He flushed. "I've mentioned you a couple times maybe."

"Why?"

"Because I like you. You're purty an' cute. Is a man supposed to be blind to that jist because he's married?"

"No, of course not, but perhaps it isn't too wise to mention it to a new wife."

"If I'd a knowed marriage was gonna put me in a straight jacket, I'd of never got married in th' first place."

"But you did get married, and a man can't just continue on the same way as before."

"She had no right to deceive me. She said when I brought her out here 'fore we was married that she loved it an' would be happy out here with me. But we wasn't married two weeks before she was naggin' me to go home. Since then she ain't stopped. I told her she could go home an' visit her folks, then she wouldn't go. I can't seem to do anything to please her. I don't know what she wants from me."

"Sounds as if she needs reassurance that you still love her," I said cooly. "Instead of that, you're clowning around with me and with Goldie and who knows who else, flirting—"

"Flirtin'!"

"Yes, flirting. Maybe you don't realize it, but you do, you know. You flirted with me at the pie supper. I don't blame her for being jealous, but I'm innocent. I have absolutely no interest in you, other than perhaps friendship, and I want you to go home and tell her that. Tell her there was nothing in it."

"It would be awful easy to fall in love with you."

"No. Don't say that. You have no right. You're a married man and I have someone waiting for me in St. Louis."

"I'm sorry."

"All right. I'm sorry too, but there's really nothing I can do to help you, it's up to you. A wife is a serious responsibility, you know. She takes a lot of care and a lot of attention. I suggest you give it to her and leave me alone. I don't want you to come back here like this again. Promise me you won't. It will only create problems for both of us."

He stood up and looked at me, his eyes doglike in their wistfulness. I tried to ignore it.

"Goodbye and I do hope things work out for you."

He held out his hand and reluctantly I put my hand in his, intending it to be a very brief handshake, but he had other ideas. He held on to my hand and I didn't like the way he was looking at me. I was afraid he was going to try to kiss me and tried to pull my hand away.

"Let her go, Jim," said a grim voice from the doorway.

He dropped my hand and whirled around. I had given a little gasp, whether of relief or of chagrin, I didn't know myself. Davy stood there, his mouth tight.

"I was jist sayin' goodbye," Jim said defensively.

"Then say it an' go."

The two of them stood there staring at one another. Jim's eyes were the first to waiver and fall, his shoulders slumped a little. He half turned to me.

" 'Bye," he said.

"Goodbye, Mr. Baker," I said, keeping my voice cool and formal.

Davy stepped aside and Jim went out. I turned back to my desk and began gathering up my papers again. The silence was pregnant with his disapproval and my resentment.

"Did you want something?" I asked. My voice sounded cold and unfriendly. It was not that I was ungrateful for his intervention, but I resented the implied censure in his attitude and bearing.

"You was late. I wondered if somethin' was wrong."

"Nothing is wrong."

"It will be though if Sally hears of this. If anybody hears of it, for that matter."

"Are you my keeper?"

"Somebody needs to be."

"I can take care of myself."

"It looks like it."

"Look, I didn't know he was coming. I certainly didn't invite him. He just came in as you did, what was I supposed to do?"

"Tell him to leave."

"I did, but he wouldn't go. Why don't you leave?"

"I'm not a married man."

"Nevertheless, your presence is annoying me."

"His evidently wasn't."

"He wanted to talk and I—well, I felt that under the

85

circumstances I should take a few minutes and explain—I asked him not to come back. Does that satisfy you?"

"Why was you holdin' his hand?"

"I wasn't and what business is it of yours?"

"You won't last long here if you keep company with married men after school hours. I thought you was really interested in stayin' here an' teachin' these kids."

"I was and I am. Will you stop sitting in judgment on me? I'm not keeping company with married men. This was the only time. I felt sorry for him."

"You're too tenderhearted. It'll get you in trouble."

I looked up, surprised. His tone was almost gentle.

"It won't happen again," I said. "I guess I'll have to come straight home after school, though it's easier to do some of my work here. Or maybe I should lock the door after the children leave, except that it won't lock on the inside."

I gathered my papers into a folder and put it under my arm, gathered up my purse, and the key to the door. He followed me outside and waited while I padlocked the door. Then he fell into step beside me.

"Let me carry them books," he said.

"No," I answered shortly, my face averted.

"Look, I didn't mean to make you mad. I was jist tryin' to show ya how it might look—"

"Oh, shut up, will you?"

We walked along in silence. I could feel him looking at me from time to time but I ignored him.

"Anne."

"Oh, go away," I cried, turning on him. "Just leave me alone, you and every other predatory male in these blasted hills. I came here," my voice wavered but I steadied it and went on, "I came here to teach school and I don't give a hang for Jim Baker or your brother Tom or you—or any one of you. All I want is for you all to stay away from me and just leave me alone!"

I glared at him, my eyes wet, my fists clenched.

"Watch your temper, teacher," he said mildly. "Has Tom been botherin' you?"

"He's only been making eyes at me behind his wife's back, that's all. You'll be blaming me for that next, I suppose."

"I wasn't blamin' you, jist tryin' ta warn you."

"I'm warned. Now will you leave me alone?"

I turned and marched on. He stayed with me and I saw a quirk of a grin on his face. It didn't improve my mood any.

"Did Calvin come to school today?" he asked after a long silence.

"Yes."

"That oughta make you happy."

"It did. I was happy as a lark until Jim came. That put a damper on my happiness. Then you came along and squashed it altogether."

"I'm sorry."

"Just stop moralizing at me, will you? I'm not a baby. I know right from wrong. I'm not a home wrecker either. Nor," I added, giving him a baleful look, "am I man-hungry."

"All right. You've made your point. Don't be so touchy."

"Touchy! Talk about touchy!"

"I'm gonna dunk you in th' crick if you don't cool down pretty quick."

I lifted my chin and sniffed haughtily and marched on up the steps onto the front porch. He went off toward his shop.

CHAPTER SIXTEEN

Dirt Poor

When I came home from
school a few days later, Clemmy had company.

She was sitting with a pan of potatoes on her lap peeling
them, and she looked up at me with an almost desperate
pleading in her eyes. I was startled, it was the first time I'd
ever seen Clemmy really perturbed.

I had heard of the woman who sat in the other rocker, but
I'd never seen her. However, because of the children, I knew
who she was.

They were absolutely beautiful little girls, identical twins
between the ages of about two and three. They were
blue-eyed with blond curly hair, but their scalps were so
encrusted with dirt, they looked as if they'd had a bleach job
and the roots had grown out. They were barefoot and
dressed in filthy rags, with dirt and food encrusted on their
faces and legs and feet. Their noses were running, they
smelled strongly of urine. I was repelled, yet fascinated,
because they seemed to be reasonably healthy and normal
children. I longed to take Clemmy's washtub down and put
them in and see what they would look like clean and
decently dressed.

I looked at their mother and involuntarily remembered
what Granny Eldridge has told me about her. She was pretty
enough, about my age, but beginning to grow heavy. She was
dressed in a long, dirty and shapeless dress. Her hair was
dark brown, stringy and oily and hanging about her face.

She sat and rocked and smiled foolishly, yet her eyes were not unintelligent. She had almost nothing to say, just seemed content to sit there and let Clemmy do all the talking. I thought she was lonely and probably very shy. The children played happily on the floor at her feet with some toys Clemmy had brought in.

I looked at the children and again Granny Eldridge's words came back to me. "She's supposed to be married to old man Simpson. He's sixty if he's a day, but they's some doubt about who th' young'uns belong to. Old man Simpson's son, Pete, lives with them. It's said she shares her favors with both men."

I was ashamed of myself for remembering that. It might or might not be true, but it was none of my business. I sat down on the floor, not too close, and thought I'd try a little test as to the children's intelligence, wondering what Clemmy wanted of me. To get rid of them probably, but how was I to do that?

I picked up a toy animal. "Cow," I said. They stared back at me. "Cow," I said again, but there was no response.

Clemmy had put some clothespins in the toys. I got a narrow-necked bottle and sat it on the floor and dropped a clothespin in. They watched, their eyes riveted to me. I dropped another one in. Suddenly one of them leaned forward, picked up a clothespin and dropped it in the bottle, then sat back with a little crow of delight. After that both of them enthusiastically played the game. They communicated with one another with an unintelligible gibberish, but I thought that was probably quite normal for twins of their age. I didn't think there was much wrong with their intelligence.

"What are their names?" I asked their mother.

"Olajean and Imogene," she answered. I wondered if she could tell them apart. I certainly couldn't.

"Anne, would you help me bring in that big pan on th'

porch?" Clemmy asked suddenly, rising up out of her chair and putting the pan of potatoes on the table.

I went out on the porch with her. She was almost ringing her hands.

"I don't know what to do," she whispered. "When she comes, she jist sets there an' stays an' stays. I didn't see her a comin' or I'd a hid. She'll be wantin' ta stay ta supper, an' Dad says he won't set down at th' table with her again. It fair turns his stomach, an' I know Davy won't either. Can't say I relish th' idee myself."

"Nor I," I admitted frankly.

"What'll I do? I don't like ta tell her ta leave."

"Could you perhaps send something home with her, some food, I mean? Tell her you know she'd like to eat with the rest of the family or something?"

"That's a idee, at least. There's them green beans an' ham on th' stove an' there's a plenty. I could save some out fer us. I could go ahead an' put th' corn bread in an' maybe send a jar of peaches. But how'd she get it home with them two young'uns?"

"I'll go with her and help."

"Bless you, child," she said, patting me, still looking distracted. "But we'll have to rush a mite. The men'll be comin' in soon."

"You get the corn bread in and I'll go down and get the peaches."

"Could you manage to pack a jar of milk too? Them young'uns don't get enough milk."

"Of course."

She rubbed her hands down the front of her apron and went back into the kitchen. I went around the side of the house and lifted the heavy cellar door. I went carefully down into the darkness and looked around at all the canned goods and produce Clemmy had stored there. The walls were lined with shelves filled with jars of canned goods. There were pumpkins and squash on the floor, bunches of onions hanging on nails on the wall, potatoes and sweet potatoes stored in crates. I took down a half gallon jar of peaches and started back up. Clemmy was putting the corn bread in the oven when I got back to the kitchen.

"I'm gonna send home a big pot of these here green beans an' ham with you," she was telling the other woman. "Th' corn bread'll be ready right quick an' I'll send some of that along with some peaches an' milk, then you can all have a nice supper together. Anne here'll go along ta help you pack it home."

She was very busy avoiding looking at her visitor and I was amused but sympathetic. It went against Clemmy's nature to be inhospitable.

"I'll get my coat," I said.

She evidently had no coat, nor did the children. It was not a really cold day, but it was chilly. I felt sorry for the poor little children with their bare feet. Our progress was slow, me with the pan of hot beans and the gallon of milk, she with the peaches and corn bread, the little ones following along behind.

I'd seen the home before, but as I stepped inside to deposit my burden, I was appalled at the squalor. It was a one-room house, the floors were dirt, the furniture consisted of an old wobbly table, a wood stove and a cabinet and three dirty pallets on the floor. The stench made me feel sick. The men were not there and I was glad.

On an impulse, I took off my coat and handed it to her. It was not my good coat and it would be small on her, but she needed it worse than I did. I didn't linger and I forgot Clemmy's dishes.

"Have a good meal," I said and rushed out into the cool air.

When I got back to the Hilton's I was out of breath and my teeth were chattering. They were already at the table.

"Where's your coat, child?" Clemmy asked.

"I gave it to her."

"Well, come an' set down."

"You go ahead. I have to wash up first."

Davy was looking at me with that look of sardonic amusement. I took the teakettle off the stove and poured hot water into the wash pan. I diluted it with a dipper of cold water and took up the bar of soap. I soaped up to my elbows and scrubbed thoroughly, then dipped water up over my face. I took a long drink and drew a deep breath. I felt a little better. When I pulled my chair out, Davy spoke.

"Thought maybe you'd decided to stay an' take supper with our neighbors," he drawled, and what little appetite I had fled. I pushed my chair back.

"I don't think I'm hungry tonight, Clemmy," I said. "Excuse me, please."

CHAPTER SEVENTEEN

Teacher's Pet

I was grading some papers at my desk, the children had all gone home, when I heard a sound at the door. I froze, afraid it might be Jim again and remembering Davy's warning. I looked around and smiled in relief. It was Calvin.

"Hello, Calvin. Did you forget something?"

He shook his head in the negative and held out a handful of papers to me. I took them and looked at them. The title on the first page was "My Pet Fox."

"Is it a story you've written, Calvin? Do you want me to read it?"

He nodded, still a child of few words.

I began to read. We had written several short stories in class such as "My Favorite Person," and "What I Did Last Summer." Calvin had shown real flair in his writing. I had made it a point to commend and encourage him, and evidently he had now decided to write a short story on his own.

As I read, Calvin stood close to me and presently he was leaning a little against me. I moved carefully, still reading, and slid my arm around him.

I think inevitably a teacher is drawn to some of her students more than to others, but I had always been very careful not to show partiality. I was certain I had not shown any marked preference for Calvin in class, but right from the start, my heart had gone out to the lonely little boy.

He came to school at the last minute and slipped in unobtrusively. He disappeared at lunchtime, then quietly slipped in again after the rest of the students were seated, and the same at recess. As soon as school was over, he was gone. However, a few times he had suddenly reappeared just as I was leaving and walked partway home with me. At those times we talked a little and were silent a lot, but it was a companionable silence. There was a rapport between us and I believe he felt it as strongly as I did. Now as I read his story, his warm little body relaxed against me, waiting calmly for my verdict.

He told about rescuing a baby red fox from some dogs that had killed its mother. He had taken it home and put it in a box with some newspapers and rags and fed it from a bottle. The name he gave it was Rusty.

As the fox grew, it began to follow him around the house. Each night when he went to bed he put Rusty in the box in his bedroom, but each morning when he woke up, the fox would be in bed with him, lying with his belly right across Calvin's neck.

He housebroke the fox, taught him tricks, but like any young puppy, Rusty liked to grab rags and shoes and such and gnaw and shake them. He began to grab at the bottoms of Granny's curtains and tug and gnaw at them until they were in shreds.

Granny was angry and whipped Rusty with a rolled-up newspaper. After that, Rusty began to lie in wait for Granny behind various pieces of furniture and when she walked by, he darted out and bit her on the backs of her ankles. Granny whipped him again for that, and Rusty did it all the more. Finally, Granny made Calvin take Rusty far out into the woods and leave him there, because she was afraid Rusty might someday turn on Calvin and bite him, perhaps on the neck or face at night while he slept. Now when Calvin went for a walk in the woods, he always kept an eye out for Rusty, and hoped someday he might see him again.

It was a warm, well-written story, except for a few misspelled words and in several instances, he had used the wrong tense. I looked at Calvin and felt almost watery-eyed.

"Calvin, it's a wonderful story," I said warmly, tightening my arm around him a little. He looked at me eagerly.

"It's very well-written. It's direct and to the point, no excess of words and a nice balance in sentence length. You've misspelled a few words here and here and here." I indicated the words with my pencil. "Also you've used the wrong tense in a few places. For instance, Calvin, we say 'we went' but not 'we had went.' With 'have,' 'has' or 'had,' we use 'gone.' We 'had gone' into the woods. And there's another place here somewhere but other than that it's an excellent story. I tell you what I'd like for you to do—"

We both looked up, startled at a sound at the door. Davy was there, his keen eyes on us. Calvin still leaned against me, my arm was still around him.

"Is something wrong?" I asked Davy rather coolly.

"Nothin' wrong. I was passin' by an' I thought I'd maybe walk on up to th' house with you."

"I'm not quite finished yet."

"I'll wait. Hullo, Cal. How you doin'?"

He sat down on the long bench. Calvin straightened and I removed my arm from around him.

"All right, Calvin," I said. "As I was saying, you've misspelled a few words."

I pointed out the words and spelled them for him while he carefully crossed out the misspelled words and wrote in the correct spelling. His tongue came out at the corner of his mouth, he was very concentrated. I watched him with affection and almost forgot the man sitting in front of us.

"Now 'gone' here, Calvin, instead of 'went,' and 'done' here instead of 'did.' "

When we were finished I looked at Davy. He raised his

brows at me and I looked back at Calvin.

"As I said, Calvin, I think it's excellent, but perhaps I'm biased. Shall we get another opinion?"

He looked at me, then at his uncle.

"Shall we let your Uncle Davy read it?"

"Okay."

I held out the manuscript. Davy rose and took it. Calvin and I waited while he read.

"I agree," Davy said when he looked up. "It's good, Cal. I remember Rusty now. Your story's brought it all back to me."

Calvin was beaming in his own quiet, withdrawn way. He took the manuscript and shuffled through it self-consciously, his head bent.

"I'd like you to rewrite it, Calvin," I said, "and do it very neatly. Then the next time I go into town, I'd like to take it to Mr. Hooper. Sometimes they publish stories written by students in the school paper, or sometimes even in the local paper. I'd like to see your story published. It might not happen, of course, but there's a chance at least. Would you like that?"

He nodded.

"Then we'll do it. Bring it back to me when you've rewritten it and keep this copy for yourself, and congratulations, Calvin. It's very good."

He made a sudden little move toward me, then turned and practically ran from the room. If Davy hadn't been there I believe he might have hugged me or even kissed me. I was quite moved.

With his departure there was silence. I moved things around unnecessarily on my desk and finally looked up at Davy. He raised his brows again.

"Teacher's pet?" he asked softly.

"Perhaps. What of it?"

"Nothin'. I think it's time poor ol' Cal had a break."

I put things away in my desk drawer, gathered up my books and rose.

"Dare I ask to carry your books today?" He asked quizzically.

I smiled. "You may ask, but I see no reason why you should carry my books. They're not heavy."

I preceded him out of the room and locked up after him. When I turned and we fell into step together, I strove to find some comfortable topic of conversation, but the words that came out were not what I intended.

"Tell me more about Calvin," I said.

He didn't answer immediately, but when he did, his words were thoughtful and without rancor.

"You're fond of Cal. You're takin' quite a interest in him. Why worry about what's over an' done with? What's that got to do with Cal anyway?"

"You're right," I agreed quickly. "I don't know why I asked, just curious, I guess. Well, have you been helping Jim on his house today?"

He glanced quickly at me and I bit my lip. Another controversial subject. What was wrong with me?

But he answered in the affirmative and began to describe the progress they were making.

CHAPTER EIGHTEEN

A Young Man Waiting

*F*all was beautiful in the hills with the leaves turning gold and red and brown, the early mornings and the evenings crisp and cool. I was thoroughly enjoying my brisk walk to and from school, satisfied with the progress I was making at school, and in general, at peace with myself and my surroundings.

November came in, cool and bright and sunny. Clemmy was planning a family celebration. It was a custom developed over the years for the family to get together the first weekend in November before winter set in. Every afternoon that week as I stepped into the kitchen after my walk home, the air was warm and redolent with the baking she was doing in preparation.

"There's something to be said for a wood fire after all," I said one afternoon, holding my hands out to the heat. "Um-m-m. Something sure smells good. What have you been baking today, Clemmy?"

"Zucchini bread an' cinnamon rolls," she answered placidly. "You kin have a roll. There's some over there on th' counter."

"Thanks, I'd love one."

I reached up for a cup and poured myself some coffee from the pot that was always on the back of the stove. I took a roll and bit into it. I caught a glimpse of myself in the wall mirror and saw that my cheeks were red from my walk, my hair was tousled from the cool breeze that was blowing. I'd

have to do something about that in a minute. I turned before
the stove to toast my back.

"Delicious, Clemmy," I said. "You must be the best cook
in the whole world. I should be fat and healthy when I leave
here. I've never eaten such food. Would you believe before I
came here I'd never even heard of zucchini bread or squash
pie or fresh pumpkin pudding? I'd never eaten rabbit stew or
fried squirrel or fried squash and onions. I'd like to have
some of your recipes before I leave, if you don't mind."

"I don't rightly use recipes."

"You don't? You mean you just do it all from memory? I
guess I'll just have to watch then. I'm determined to learn to
make biscuits like yours."

"Why don't you ask her for her recipe for possum?"

It was the dry drawling voice of Davy. He came in from
the living room, eyebrows raised and a quirk of a grin on his
lips.

I glanced quickly at Clemmy. She was rolling pieces of
chicken in flour. "I'm afraid I don't care much for possum,"
I said carefully. "I've learned to like turnips and even turnip
greens, and I love fried squash, but you can keep the possum,
thanks."

"I'm not right fond of possum myself," Clemmy said. She
raised her head and gave me an almost arch look, reminiscent of her son.

"It's so—slick," I said, with a little shudder. "Besides, I
doubt I'll have much opportunity to cook possum when I get
back to town."

"Ever eaten persimmons?" Davy asked, helping himself to
coffee and a roll.

"Persimmons? No, I haven't."

"Try one."

He took the cloth off a box of small apricot-colored fruit. I
took one and examined it.

"I don't think I've ever seen one before," I said.

"Now don't you pull one of your tricks on her," Clemmy admonished.

"Tricks?"

"I wouldn't do that, but it's jist as well you be warned. Persimmons ain't fit to eat 'til after a good frost. They should be soft and wrinkled like these. If you pick them too early an' bite into one, you'll be puckered up for a week. Go ahead an' try it."

I looked from him to his mother. "Is this one all right?" I asked.

"Don't you trust me?"

"Not particularly."

Clemmy looked at the persimmon and nodded. I cautiously bit into it.

"Well?"

"It's mostly seeds."

"Yes, but how do you like th' taste?"

"It's good."

"Mom makes jam out of it an' puts it in ice cream, an' even makes persimmon bread. It's good."

"I'll bet it is, but it must be a lot of work getting all those seeds out. You know, coming out here has been almost like going to a foreign country, with all kinds of strange and exotic foods and customs. I almost need to come back next year to be able to absorb it all."

"Why don't you?"

"Other commitments."

"Oh yeah, th' young man waitin' in St. Louis," he said.

"I thought I might take some more college courses too. I'd like to pursue my music a little further."

"While I'm thinkin' of it, I got a message for you."

"A message?"

"From Jim."

I glanced apprehensively at Clemmy. She seemed engrossed in her work.

"What sort of message?"

"He said tell you he took your advice. He an' Sally are movin' to town for th' winter and takin' a place somewhere near her family. He's takin' a temporary job in her dad's warehouse, an' they'll be comin' back here in th' spring. He wants me to finish up his house for him."

I gave a sigh of relief. "I'm so glad. I hope things work out for them."

"He said tell you thanks."

"And what do you have to tell me?" I challenged, low-voiced.

"Me?"

"Yes, you. Don't you think you owe me an apology?"

"What for?"

"For your suspicions."

"What suspicions?"

I gave him a look of scorn and turned away.

"Anything I can help with, Clemmy?" I asked.

"Not yet. Are you stayin' this weekend?"

"What do you want me to do? You'll have a big crowd here."

"It'd be a chance for you to meet some more of th' kids' folks."

"Is it just family, Clemmy?"

"Mostly, but others drop in too. They'll be wantin' to see Al an' his family an' th' girls, if they come."

I was wondering if she was thinking of the daughter who was Calvin's mother. I'd heard that she hadn't been seen or heard from for several years.

"Do you think," I asked rather hesitantly, "it would be all right if I invited my folks? Just my mom and dad? They've been wanting to come and I'd like for them to meet you and some of my students. They probably wouldn't stay more than a couple of hours."

"I think that would be right nice."

I had no doubt of the sincerity of that statement. Her face was beaming at me with pleasure. With Clemmy it was a case of the more the merrier, I thought.

"What about your young man?" Davy asked.

For some reason, I blushed. "Good idea," I said, giving him a challenging look. "I'll invite him too. I'd better drive over to the Miller's and phone them. They'll need a few days notice. What can they bring, Clemmy? How about a big stack of paper plates and cups? That would save a lot of washing up."

That settled, I prepared to drive to the Miller's, a farm family that lived just off the main highway, where we picked up our mail and made any necessary phone calls when we didn't want to drive on into town.

My folks were pleased and said they'd come on Saturday about noon. They'd pass the message on to Don Bradford, who was the young man I had mentioned. I had mixed emotions as to whether I wanted him to accept the invitation or not.

Saturday turned out to be a fine fall day. The early morning air was crisp and cool, but the sun shone brightly. The two Hilton sons who still lived there in the hills, Brad and Tom, arrived early with their families. Under Clemmy's supervision, the men set up long tables made of boards and sawhorses in the side yard. The kitchen was hot and fragrant with the ham in the oven, the chicken frying on the stove. I went around trying to make myself generally useful. I carried out platter after platter of food and the children were assigned to stand guard to keep the dogs and chickens away. More than once, I saw a small hand reach out stealthily to the table as a child walked innocently by.

By noon some forty people had assembled. The yard was a bustle of activity. I kept an eye out for my parents as I moved among the people, meeting more of the Hilton family, greeting many of my students.

I saw them drive up in a flashy red car, three people in the front seat, and had a moment of wishing they'd come in my parents' old station wagon. I ran to meet them, hugging my father first since he was the first to get out. Then came my mother and I clung to her for a minute. Mom and I had always been very close. Lastly, I turned to the younger man who came around the car and smiled demurely, holding out my hand to him. He took my hand, but pulled me toward him and kissed me on the cheek.

"I'm so glad you could come," I said happily. "Come and meet everyone."

"Everyone?" asked the young man, blinking his eyes as he looked around at all the people. "Get away, dog."

"Down, Bouncer," I commanded. "Well, maybe not everyone, but at least Clemmy and Willy Hilton."

"Will my car be all right here?"

"It'll be fine."

He cast an anxious eye around at the kids and dogs and chickens before he fell in step with the rest of us. Mom had brought a cake besides the stack of paper plates and cups. We deposited these at the end of the improvised table, and I turned to introduce my parents to Clemmy who was approaching. Everyone else seemed to have fallen strangely quiet, staring at the strangers. It made me a little nervous. I hoped they didn't feel we were intruding.

"Clemmy, I want you to meet my parents, Marsha and James Davis, and this is Don Bradford."

They shook hands and exchanged greetings. Clemmy didn't hug anyone as she'd hugged me that first time, but she beamed with hospitality. Mom right away thanked her for looking after me so well, as if I'd been a child. Dad and Don stood off a little uneasily, looking around at the people and the surroundings.

Davy rather surprised me by breaking away from his brothers and coming to join us. He seemed relaxed and at ease. I introduced him first to Mom.

Mom smiled up at him and even patted his arm as she

shook his hand. He retained her hand for a moment, responding immediately to her warmth.

"I was telling your mother how well Anne looks," she told him, "and no wonder. It's beautiful out here and so peaceful. And the smell of all that food. It's heavenly. I'm not surprised Anne looks so well."

"She seems to be settlin' in pretty good," he drawled, his eyes twinkling, his lips smiling down at her. "We had a little trouble with her at first, but I think we got her pretty much in line now."

"You and who else?" I retorted without thinking.

"Almost in line," he amended, still looking at Mom. "You folks are jist in time. I think we're ready to eat. The kids are starvin'."

I introduced Dad and Don and the men shook hands, measuring each other with their eyes rather warily, I thought. Davy took Mom's arm and went toward the table and I followed along with Don and Dad. Clemmy had already bustled off.

"What's he talking about, he's got you in line?" Don demanded low-voiced.

"Sh-h-h," I said.

The food was plentiful and delicious, but many of the dishes were strange to my parents and Don. Mom sampled everything, but Dad and Don took only the conventional foods. I stayed close to Dad, and Don stayed close to me. Mom mingled as she always did. I'd never seen her look out of place wherever she was. She was a real genteel and gentle lady. I wished I could be more like her.

I found my eyes going repeatedly to Davy's brother John and his wife Carrie. John was the carpenter brother who lived in town and that Davy sometimes worked with. I liked what I saw. He was quiet and good-natured, she was fat and jolly and rather lazy, I suspected. Their children were grown up, only one of them having shown up for the get-together. They were obviously more affluent than most of the others. I thought sometime I'd have a private talk with Carrie and John about Calvin.

Don stood before me. "Go for a walk?" he asked.

"All right," I said.

I took him down toward the creek, his arm thrown across my shoulders. I made no attempt to remove his arm, just as well let everyone believe I actually was committed to him. I had been kept busy avoiding the intent gray eyes of Tom Hilton. His wife was right there, a quiet, nice appearing person, but it seemed to make no difference. Tom Hilton had roving eyes, and he seemed to be trying to make contact with me. I was a little afraid of him.

I dismissed Tom from my mind, and thought instead of Calvin. He should be here, I thought. It's not fair that he isn't.

"Why so solemn?" Don asked.

"Just thinking."

"About what? About whom, maybe I should say."

"About one of my students."

"Sure?"

"Sure. Why?"

"Just wondered." We had stopped. He released me and hooked his thumbs in his pockets. "This guy, Davy. Isn't he the one you had trouble with when you first came here?"

"Yes, but we're friends now. It was just a misunderstanding."

"You like him?"

"Yes, I like him all right."

"And he likes you?"

"I have no idea. He tolerates me. Why?"

"Just wondered. Seems to me he watches you a lot."

"You're imagining things."

"Maybe. So, you like it here?"

"I love it. Don't you?"

"Um-m, but rustic, isn't it?"

"So, what's wrong with rustic?"

"Nothing, if you like that sort of thing." He turned back to me and took hold of my arms. "Still love me?" he asked.

I smiled up at him. "Yes, as a brother, or perhaps a cousin," I answered.

"Absence hasn't made the heart grow fonder?"

"Don, I'll always be fond of you, we've known each other for such a long time, but no, absence hasn't made the heart grow fonder."

"There's no hope for me then?"

"Don, please. You don't love me, you've just gotten into the habit of thinking you do. Can't we forget all this and just be friends?"

He sighed and released me. "When you left to come out here, I told you I'd wait for you."

"And I told you not to," I reminded gently.

"I know, but I hoped—it looks like I hoped in vain."

"I'm sorry."

"Ah, well," he said and shrugged, looking off across the creek. "Is there anyone else? This guy Davy, maybe?"

"Davy? Heavens no, there's no one, Don."

"Then—"

"No, Don, don't. I don't love you that way. I'm sorry. I think maybe I was meant to be an old maid teacher and devote myself to my students."

"Yeah, sure," he answered.

"I just might. We'd better get back, Don. Are you going back tonight?"

"Your folks wanted to stay with their friends in town and go home tomorrow afternoon, so I guess we'll do that. Are you coming back to town with us? I think your folks are hoping you will."

"All right, I will."

"Maybe you'll go out with me tonight?"

"Yes, I'd like that. I haven't been out with anyone since I've been here."

"That's a bit unusual for you, isn't it?"

"I must be losing my touch," I said lightly. "Nobody has asked me."

"Anne," he said and there was a note in his voice that brought my head up. He chose that moment to bend and kiss me. Out of the corner of my eye, I saw Davy off in the distance carrying a covered plate in each hand. I know he saw Don kissing me. Perhaps it was just as well, it would help to further the myth that I was committed. I felt I needed that protection.

We stayed only a short time after that. I made sure my parents met Willy Hilton, then the four of us walked to the schoolhouse and I showed them around.

Mom was interested in everything and uncritical. Dad, I could see, was faintly appalled at the backwoods atmosphere and primitiveness. Don said little, but his feelings, I thought were very much like Dad's.

I didn't feel too bad about Don. I didn't think his feelings were as deeply involved as he thought. Anyhow, we were much too different in outlook, in our likes and dislikes. It was not the kind of relationship that would have brought either of us happiness.

When we left for town, Mom and Dad went in my car and I rode with Don. The festivities were still in full swing at the Hilton's.

CHAPTER NINETEEN

A Chance for Calvin

Before they left for home, Mom took me aside for a minute. I could see she was worried.

"Anne," she said, "about Don. When you left, I thought that was over, but the fact that you invited him out here and went out with him last night, does that mean —?"

"It doesn't mean anything, Mom."

"You're twenty-four years old, dear, and I have no right to interfere, but —"

"But what, Mom? What's worrying you?"

"You know I like Don, but he wouldn't be the sort who's easy to live with. Your interests are so much in contrast, you're so spontaneous and outgoing, and he has a tendency to be rather critical, you know."

"Mom, stop worrying. I'm not involved with Don except as a friend."

I went and sat on the bed beside her and put my arm around her.

"I want you to be happy, Anne," she said, still worried. "It's so easy to make a mistake, so easy to get involved with the wrong person. He can, or she can, even be a very good and worthwhile person, but still be the wrong person."

"Mom," I said again, my heart going out to her. She should know, she'd had that kind of marriage herself, but she had stuck with it and it had perhaps made her a better person, though not an entirely happy person. Don was very much like Dad, and she was telling me he wouldn't be a good match for me. She wanted me to find the happiness and compatibility in marriage that she hadn't found.

"If you won't rat on me, I'll tell you why I invited Don out," I teased gently. Mom had always been the kind of mother that I could talk to with perfect confidence.

I told her about Davy's initial reaction to me and the basic reason, without going into a lot of detail. I also told her about the little episode with Jim Baker, and that was when Don and his promise to wait for me came to my aid. Perhaps I was using him to a certain extent, but it wouldn't hurt him. I didn't mention Tom Hilton, afraid it might really worry her.

"And you've told him you won't marry him?" Mom asked, still anxious.

"Yes, Mom, and I think he's finally accepted it. That was one of the reasons I invited him out, to get that cleared up, but mostly to show Davy Hilton that he wasn't a myth."

"Why Davy Hilton?"

I was a little confused and glanced away.

"Because he—well, if he believes it, the others will too. He has a lot of influence with the rest of the family, and Jim Baker is a good friend of his."

"I liked that young man, Davy, I mean. I think he'd make a very loyal friend."

"He liked you too, Mom. I could tell it. Davy's not usually too outgoing, he's fairly reserved and quiet. What did you think of Clemmy?"

We talked a few more minutes, then they left, and I got in my own car. Earlier I had looked up a certain name in the phone book and jotted down the address and consulted a city map. I had two stops I wanted to make before I headed back to the hills.

I went to see Mr. Hooper, and found that Calvin's story about his pet fox would be published in the next week or so in the local paper. Mr. Hooper would save me two issues of that paper. I discussed Luther with him, because Luther was missing a lot of school and I would have no choice but to fail him again.

Next, I drove to a middle-class neighborhood to a modest, well-kept house. When I knocked on the door, it was opened by a jolly familiar person.

"Hello, Mrs. Hilton," I said.

"Why, hello. What brings you here?"

"I wondered if I might talk to you and your husband for a few minutes."

"My husband isn't home right now, but come on in. I was just going to have a cup of coffee. Will you have one with me?"

"Thanks."

I sat down in a comfortable chair and looked around while she went for the coffee. The room was comfortable and homey, but not overly neat. It reminded me very much of its mistress.

I took the cup held out to me and thanked her. She lowered her bulk carefully into an overstuffed chair and looked frankly at me.

"The parents and boyfriend off to St. Louis?" she asked.

"Yes, and I'm headed back to the cabin, but I decided to take a chance of finding you and your husband home. I wanted to talk to you about—well, about a subject that is forbidden in your father-in-law's house."

"Calvin?"

"Yes. How did you know?"

"Davy's told us about your interest in the boy."

"Then I gather the subject's not forbidden in your house?"

"No, why should it be?"

"Mrs. Hilton."

"Call me Carrie."

"All right Carrie. I brought some of Calvin's work with me. I wanted you and your husband to look it over. Since he's not here, could I just leave it?"

"With what purpose?"

"Calvin has a gift, Mrs. Hilton, I mean Carrie, a gift for words, for writing stories. He writes constantly, he reads constantly. As you can see, he has trouble with grammar and punctuation and with tenses, but that can be overcome. I want him to have his chance, to have an education so he can develop his talent. I want him to go to high school, maybe even to college."

Carrie just looked at me, her eyebrows raised. She didn't look at Calvin's papers. I continued.

"I know he's only in fourth grade. He's two years behind because he dropped out for awhile, but in many ways he's more advanced than the other fourth graders. With a little extra effort, he could be ready for sixth grade next year, and then in two more years, ready for high school. I know his chances of going are pretty slim, but I wanted to ask you and your husband if—well, if you'd help him get to high school."

"How?"

"Could you perhaps have him to stay here with you? Davy said he stayed with you a year while he went to ninth grade."

She was silent again. I finished my coffee and rose.

"I don't expect an answer now. I just want you to be thinking about it. Calvin deserves his chance, he needs it, and somebody needs to care enough to help him."

"Quite a few people care, actually," she said mildly. "His Grandma Hilton cares, and Davy cares. They keep an eye on him. Didn't you see the two plates Clemmy heaped up yesterday and Davy took around the corner?"

Were they for Granny and Calvin, I wondered? "But Carrie," I continued on, "an education is so important for Calvin, what future does he have without it?"

"Probably about the same as everyone else."

"Maybe. Maybe not. Will you at least discuss it with your husband?"

"Sure. Why not?"

"Thank you, and thank you for the coffee. Don't get up, I'll let myself out."

"I'll probably be seeing you around," she said. "If you ever want to come in with Davy, come ahead."

"Thanks, I might do that. 'Bye."

" 'Bye."

I let myself out and walked back to my car, not knowing if I had accomplished anything or not.

CHAPTER TWENTY

A Crusading Spirit

Winter closed in on the hills, the days grew shorter. I found myself walking to school while it was barely daylight, but the wood furnace was always burning, the schoolroom warm, at least in the vicinity of the stove where the little ones sat. I learned to wear warm skirts and layers of sweaters and sensible shoes. It was a little drafty where my desk was.

The cloak room was always full of boots and coats and scarves. Some of the children had quite a distance to walk and, on occasion, the little Proctor girls were driven in by their father in an open wagon drawn by a team of mules. Their little faces were blue and pinched with cold. They were very poor and shabbily clothed and sometimes had no more than a biscuit for lunch. My heart went out to them and with Clemmy's consent, I began taking extra for my own lunch and sharing with them.

There were others who were poor also and barely had adequate clothing for the cold weather. Some seemed to have perpetual colds with runny noses and coughs, and the closed-in room often reeked with unwashed bodies. I tried not to be offended by it, but I always opened some windows and aired the room thoroughly each afternoon after school. If there was only some way I could help in a more tangible way, perhaps get some of the more prosperous families together and see if they couldn't help the less fortunate ones. I needed to discuss it with someone, but who? Clemmy was the very personification of kindness and hospitality but she was already overworked trying to help her own family. Mr. Hooper might have some ideas, but he probably wouldn't be able to offer much help either. It would have to be Davy.

So one evening after the older Hiltons had gone to bed and Davy was sitting by the kitchen stove reading, I decided now was the time. I sat at the table, books and papers spread out before me, a kerosene lamp casting flickering shadows across the pages. The door was closed between kitchen and living room because the older Hiltons liked to leave their bedroom door open to get some of the heat from the living room stove and didn't want to be disturbed by my light. It was an oddly intimate scene with Davy sitting by the stove, me at the table. I glanced over at him just as he raised his eyes and looked at me. We both smiled. We had become friends.

"Could I talk to you?" I asked.

"Sure."

I smiled again, impishly. "You forget to say 'again?' "

He grinned and obliged. "Again?" he sighed in mock exasperation.

"Yes, again. I need some advice and you're elected."

He put his book down, uncrossed his legs and rose. "Maybe I better fortify myself for this," he said, rummaging in the cupboard. He brought out a sack of peanuts and shelled some into a bowl, then took down a can of sorghum and mixed some of it in with the raw peanuts.

"That's a favorite snack with you, isn't it?"

"It's good. Want some?"

"No, thanks."

He walked over to me and held a spoonful to my mouth. "Try it," he said.

I opened my mouth and took the bite. He sat back down, recrossed his legs and took a bite himself. I had to chew awhile before I could swallow and speak again.

"It is good. Should be a nourishing snack for children,

which is what I wanted to talk to you about."

"What? Sorghum an' peanuts?"

"No, silly, undernourished children. So many of the children have colds all the time, I don't think they're getting fed properly, they need fruit and juices."

I went over and drew the other rocker up close to the stove and leaned forward.

"Davy, I know some of them don't have adequate food, the little Proctor girls, for instance. They're so poor and underfed and underclothed, and there are others too. The Andersons, the Lovettes. Why doesn't someone help them? Some of the other families surely have outgrown clothing they could pass on, food they could share."

He looked down at the dish in his hand. "You're makin' me feel guilty," he said mournfully.

"I'm sorry, I didn't mean—"

While I was in midsentence he popped another spoonful of peanuts and sorghum in my mouth, stopping me very effectively. He grinned and finished off his snack.

"Partners in crime," he drawled, putting the empty bowl on the counter.

"Seriously, Davy—"

"Don't talk with your mouth full."

I finished chewing and swallowed. "Don't you want to talk about it?" I asked, a little disturbed.

He sighed. "Crusadin' female teachers," he said. "Okay, shoot. I'm listenin'."

"That's about it, Davy. It's heartbreaking to see how poor some of them are. Do you think as teacher I might organize something to help them?"

"It's not your job, teacher. It might be resented by some an' taken advantage of by others."

"What do you mean?"

"Th' Andersons get help from th' gover'ment, A.D.C."

"Then why aren't the children better provided for?"

"You tell me, but you can see why others are reluctant to help, can't you?"

"I suppose so, but the children shouldn't have to suffer because of the parents' mismanagement."

"Ain't that always th' way it is? Try helpin' them, an' see what happens. You'll find ol' man Anderson campin' on your doorstep and doin' even less than he does now to help his family."

"What about the Proctors, and the Lovettes?"

"Don't know much about th' Proctors, seen him a couple times is all, he's not talkative. They keep to theirselves, ain't been here too long. The Lovettes are pretty much th' same as th' Andersons."

"Then you don't think anything can be done?"

"Might mention it to Mom an' I got a sister-in-law with somethin' of a crusadin' spirit too. They might get some things together. What do they need, boots, coats?"

"Everything, I'd say, but I hate to bother your mother, she does so much already."

"Maybe Ellen'll do the fetchin' and deliverin'."

"Ellen?"

"My sister-in-law, Tom's wife."

"Oh. I didn't hear her name, I guess. She's very—quiet, so I didn't get too well acquainted with her at the get-together."

"You was too busy avoidin' Tom."

Surprised, I looked at him and quickly away.

"Well, then, I'll mention it to your mother and maybe she can pass it on to your sister-in-law."

"What else, teacher?"

"What else?"

"Was there somethin' else you wanted to talk to me about?"

I looked back at him and hesitated, unsure of how to proceed.

"Well?"

"I think we need some classes on proper nutrition and even some instruction on hygiene."

"For th' kids or th' parents?"

"Both, I think."

"Instruct th' kids, but forget th' parents."

"Why?"

"They wouldn't appreciate it. You're here to teach th' kids and they tolerate you, even respect you for that. You're not here to teach them how to take care of their kids an' how to feed them. That would make you a interferin' busybody."

"Why? Lots of schools and charitable organizations offer evening classes to adults on nutrition and family planning and such things. Why couldn't I do that here?"

"Maybe you could if you lived here an' they felt you was one of them, an' if you was married an' had kids of your own. Then they might feel you knew what you was talkin' about."

I looked at him resentfully. "Then, according to your opinion, there's nothing at all I can do?"

"Go ahead an' teach th' kids about hygiene an' nutrition if you want to. You might accomplish somethin' for th' next generation."

"I suppose that's all I can do. There's some instruction required on hygiene and nutrition anyhow, maybe I could enlarge on it. Well, thanks," I said, rising on a sigh.

"Thanks for nothin', huh?" he said with a grin.

He went back to his book and I went back to my schoolwork laid out on the table. He said good night to me at about ten-thirty and went out to his shop. I went to bed soon afterward.

The next morning when I entered the schoolhouse, there was an open box of peanuts near the door, with a note attached.

"Should I have included a can of sorghum, teacher?" it said.

Toward the end of the week, Clemmy and Ellen Hilton had collected together two boxes of clothing and Ellen brought them to the schoolhouse on Friday. She and I distributed them by size and need to the children and I sent a note home to the parents. I never heard back from any of them, but it was a relief and a satisfaction to see them dressed more warmly. I liked Ellen Hilton very much and wondered why she put up with a husband like Tom. I felt self-conscious with her and a little guilty and was angry with myself for those feelings.

CHAPTER TWENTY-ONE

The First Snow

*T*he first snowfall came late on a Monday afternoon, drifting down in large lazy flakes, cloaking the hills in white silence. I stood at the kitchen window watching, almost spellbound, it was so very beautiful.

I turned to Clemmy. Supper was over, the dishes were cleared away, it wouldn't be long before she and her husband would be going to bed. She had one more chore, straining the milk and washing the milk bucket, then her work for the day would be over. Mr. Hilton or Davy had not come in yet to get the milk bucket, so Clemmy sat down heavily in her rocker. She was always tired at the end of her long, busy day.

"Clemmy, I want to go out in the snow," I said almost breathlessly, thinking humorously that I sounded like an eager child seeking permission from her mother. "What can I do? Shut up the hen house? Bring in more wood?"

"You can get a few arm-loads of wood, if you've a mind to," she returned, "and stack it there on th' side porch. Knock th' snow off first."

I pulled on my sturdy, sensible boots, my coat and gloves and wrapped a warm scarf around my head and neck. I went out and stood in the yard, my head lifted so that the soft flakes fell on my face and melted away. My shoulders and arms were soon covered.

I made three trips up on the porch with my arms loaded with firewood. On the third trip, Davy stuck his head out of his shop door and called to me to bring the milk bucket.

"Clemmy, can you hand me the milk bucket for Davy?" I asked through a crack in the door. "I can't come in, I'm all covered with snow, and if you want to go on to bed, I'll take care of the milk for you."

I made my way toward the shop, milk bucket in hand, and Davy met me halfway. It was beginning to grow dusky.

"Think you're Snow White or somethin'?" Davy teased, taking the bucket.

"Isn't it a gorgeous sight?" I asked him. "Everything so still, so peaceful. It does something to me."

"It'll do somethin' to you in th' mornin' if it keeps on, 'specially if th' wind picks up, an' it drifts."

I looked at him with disgust.

"Do you have to be so down-to-earth, so literal about everything? Have you no romance in your soul?"

"Romance?"

"What's that?" I mocked and he reached out and flicked the snow off the front of my hair.

"Too bad your fella ain't here. Would he like it, do you think?"

"How could anyone help but love it?"

"He struck me as bein' a strictly city slicker."

"Doesn't mean he couldn't enjoy a country night like this. Can I come with you? I've only been to the barn one time with your mother. I'd like to see the baby pigs again."

"Come ahead. Maybe you'd like to try your hand at milkin'?"

It was almost dark in the barn, there was the smell of hay and animals, the stamp of an impatient hoof, the soft grunting sound of the baby pigs. I stood silent just inside the door while Davy hung the milk bucket on a nail and took a lantern down and lit it.

"This way, Snow White."

He went up a few steps to the center of the barn and held

the door for me. We were inside a slightly elevated, enclosed area that separated the stalls on either side.

"Ever seen a possum?"

"No. Is—there one here?"

"Relax, he's in a pen. Come look."

He held the lantern and two eyes glowed out at me. I went closer to have a better look.

"May I ask why you have a possum here? He's not a pet, surely."

"Mom won't cook them right after they're caught. She says they're dirty 'cause they eat other dead animals. So Dad has to catch them alive an' keep them penned up for a month or so an' feed them corn an' vegetables before Mom'll cook them for him."

"If I didn't like possum before, I certainly wouldn't like it now. He looks too much like a big fat rat to me."

"He's a relative of th' kangaroo, actually."

"Kangaroo meat doesn't appeal to me either, I'm afraid."

"Want to wait here or go on up in th' loft with me?"

"I'll go up, please. You go ahead. I'll just follow."

"Hang onto th' rail."

I followed him up steep narrow steps. He was hanging the lantern on a hook, and it swayed gently to and fro, casting shadows across his face. I stepped forward and he put out a hand to stop me.

"Look a little to your left there, teacher," he said, pointing.

"What is it?"

"A hole. Step in it an' you'll find yourself down in Shorty's manger."

"Oh."

"Stay put a minute, then I'll show you somethin'."

I stayed put while he lifted forkfuls of pungent hay and pushed them through the line of holes that I could dimly perceive along the left side of the loft. Then he stuck the fork back in the mound of hay and went along closing down trap doors across the holes. He took the lantern down and held his hand out to me.

"What is it?" I asked.

"Climb up that hay there an' I'll show you."

We climbed up together. He soon let go of my hand, he had to be very careful with the lantern.

"Watch your head," he said, as we neared the rafters. We were almost against the roof along the west wall when we stopped with barely enough room to sit.

"Look," he said, holding the lantern before him.

I looked and saw a gray striped mother cat lying on her side in a small indenture with several tiny, furry kittens attached to her, nursing.

"Oh, how sweet," I murmured. "They're so tiny. How old are they?"

"Jist a few days." His big hand reached out and gently detached one of them and handed it to me. "See, their eyes ain't open yet."

I cradled the kitten in the palm of my hand. I had earlier removed my gloves and put them in my pocket, now the kitten felt soft and warm in my hand, its little head bobbing up and down, eyes pasted shut. I stroked its head and back with my fingers. The mother cat looked on, unperturbed.

"They're all the same color. How many? Five? What will you do with them?"

"If we can't give 'em away, drown 'em."

"Davy Hilton, you wouldn't. That's cruel."

"How many you want then?"

"Could I have one?"

"Have 'em all if you want to."

"Well, of course, I couldn't take them all, but I might take one, a boy, I think. Can I come back in daylight and pick one out?"

"Watch out for th' trap doors, I don't always shut them, and don't think you can come out an' pet th' baby pigs like you can th' kittens. That ol' sow would eat you alive. Stay away from her."

"Okay."

I put the kitten back, stroked the other tiny furry bodies, then the mother cat. She began to purr with pleasure.

"Ever been in a hayloft with a tin roof when it's rainin'?" asked Davy.

"I've never been in a hayloft before, period."

"You city folks sure miss out on a lot of fun."

"You may be right. What's so special about a hayloft with a tin roof when it's raining?"

"There's nothin' like it, for daydreamin' or even for sleepin'. Next time it rains, you oughta come up an' try it."

"I'd like to. Did you build this barn? It's unusually fine. Most I've seen look as if a strong wind would bring them tumbling down."

"Me an' John built it mostly. Tom an' Brad helped. Ready?"

"If you are."

We scrambled back down to the floor and down the stairs. Davy hung the lantern on another hook suspended from a rafter. I could see the heads of several mules and horses and two cows, and hear them munching on the hay. The sow rose with a loud grunt sending the pigs away, squealing. Davy threw several ears of corn to her. She was on the one side of the barn, separated from the other pigs by wooden gates. The baby pigs were darling, they had grown considerably since I'd seen them a few weeks earlier.

Davy gave the four mules and the two horses a few ears of corn each. For the cows, he took the shuck off and broke each ear in half. I asked him why.

"The pigs an' horses an' mules bite th' corn off th' cob, but a cow takes th' whole thing in her mouth, then spits th' cob out. They have to be broke in two, otherwise they'd choke her."

"Oh. Is there anything I can do?"

"It's all done, 'cept th' milkin'. Wanna try your hand at that?"

"I don't know."

"Come on. I'll show you."

He only milked one cow, there was a new calf with the other one. I was able to reach out and stroke it through the wood bars.

The milk was streaming into the bucket under Davy's hands. I watched the milk foaming up, and saw cats begin to appear from all directions. Davy lifted his brows at me.

"Still think drownin' baby kittens is such a cruel thing?" he challenged.

"Good grief," I said.

He poured milk into a flat tin pan and there were at least a dozen cats around the pan immediately, including the new mother. Davy didn't sit down beside the cow again, but handed the one-legged stool to me.

"Try it," he said.

I took the stool doubtfully. It was just a short board about four inches wide nailed to a one-foot high two-by-four. I put it down beside the cow and held it and gingerly lowered myself on it. I promptly lost my balance and would have toppled backward if Davy hadn't caught me.

"Put it back a little, then lean a little forward," he instructed. "Now take the bucket between your knees—"

"Easy for you to say. You don't have to wear a dress," I grumbled, pushing my skirt back to make a place for the bucket. Fortunately, I had on a full skirt.

"Now, lean your forehead against th' cow, here. Let go of th' bucket and take hold of th' teats."

When I took my hand from the bucket, it slipped. I had to readjust it, and then gripped it more tightly between my knees.

"I hope this is a patient cow," I said.

"She'll stand here for hours so long as she's got food in her stall. Now take hold of th' teats an' squeeze, startin' at th' top."

I tried to do as he said but nothing happened, except the cow moved and I almost lost my balance again.

"Let go," Davy said patiently, "an' start again. Jist take hold with your thumbs an' top finger. Now squeeze, an' gradually go down, like this, one hand, then th' other." He squatted beside me and showed me. A long, white stream of milk squirted down in the bucket, then another. I sighed and tried again. After my third attempt, a little trickle of milk appeared. I kept doggedly trying until I was actually milking the cow. When I rose, my hands were cramping, my arms limp with fatigue.

"Whew," I said. "Who'd ever have thought milking a cow could be so hard! It looks so easy when you do it."

"It is easy, once you learn how."

He made short work of the rest of the milking, rose in one fluid movement, the bucket in one hand, the stool in the other. He put the stool on a shelf, blew the lantern out and we left the barn.

It was still snowing heavily, there must have been a good three inches on the ground already. We walked back to the house in companionable silence.

"Cold?" he asked.

"Not really."

"Want to carry in more wood? Th' snow will get it all wet."

"All right."

He took the milk on up to the house, I went to the wood pile. He rejoined me and we carried wood and stacked it all along the inside wall of the side porch. When he decided it was enough, we brushed ourselves off and went into the kitchen. Clemmy was just washing out the milk bucket.

"Brad brought th' mail by," she said, nodding toward the table.

"Anything for me?" I asked.

"Couple of letters."

Davy and I took turns washing up. Clemmy went on to bed, closing the kitchen door behind her. Mr. Hilton had either already gone to bed, or hadn't come in yet. I took up my letters, one from Mom and one from my oldest sister. Davy began sorting out the newspapers.

I read my letters, sitting before the stove in one rocker, Davy in the other.

"Mom says hello," I said once, otherwise there was silence.

"Here's somethin' you'll be interested in," Davy said out of the silence.

I raised my head. "What is it?"

"Come see."

I went and bent over beside him and looked where he indicated. It was Calvin's story.

"Oh," I exclaimed happily, suddenly kneeling beside his chair and clasping both my hands around his arm. "They did print it. Mr. Hooper said they'd promised they would. Isn't it wonderful? 'My Pet Fox, by Calvin Eldridge.' My dear little Calvin's name in print. I can't wait to see his face."

As I looked up, Davy's own face was close, his expression odd. I glanced down and realizing I was hugging his arm close to me, I blushed and released him and rose.

"I'm sorry. I got carried away. May I have it to show Calvin? I'll bring it back. Mr. Hooper promised he'd save me a couple of copies, but I'd like Calvin to see it right away."

He detached that section and handed it silently to me. I read it over. They had printed it exactly as written. It was just a small local paper, but that didn't diminish my pleasure. Calvin was on his way, I felt sure of it.

Davy left soon after that and I went to bed, happy in my expectations for tomorrow.

CHAPTER TWENTY-TWO

Shot and Butchered

*T*he radio said we had five inches of snow on the ground. It was a beautiful morning, not a cloud in the sky, the sun dazzling on the snow. There had been no wind so there was no drifting as Davy had so pessimistically predicted. Still I found it fairly hard-going wading my way to school, in spite of the fact that Davy had gone that way earlier and had more or less cleared a path for me.

I had less than a third of my students there that day, only the ones who lived fairly close had braved the weather with one exception. The little Proctor girls were driven in by their father, sitting huddled together under a blanket in the back of the wagon, their little faces red and pinched with cold.

Calvin was there. I lost no time in showing him the article and he carried it to his seat bemused, and sat looking at it for a very long time. Later with his permission, I read the story to the other children. Some of them may have been impressed, some were not.

It was a pleasant, relaxed day. At recess, I took hold of Calvin and persuaded him to stay. We all dressed warmly and went outside to play in the snow. We made a huge snowman. Calvin took part and no one treated him any different than anyone else. I hoped it was a real break-through and he would finally be accepted as just another child.

By noon it had warmed up considerably and the snow began to melt. Our snowman shrunk and finally toppled over. When we started home, there was more mud than snow. Calvin walked partway with me, holding my hand and swinging it a little. We didn't talk and when we were nearly in sight of the cabin, he released my hand and darted off, back in the direction we had come. I went on up to the cabin, feeling lighthearted and happy. My boots were muddy. I stopped to remove them before I went inside and was aware of raised voices in the kitchen. That was unusual and made me hesitant to open the door. When I did, there was instant silence. I looked from Mr. Hilton to Clemmy to Davy who stood like a ramrod, his jaw tight, his eyes cold and hard.

"Is something—wrong?" I quavered, feeling I must be the culprit. I cast about desperately in my mind in that instant before Davy answered and decided Mr. Hilton must have found out about my interest in Calvin. Was I about to be kicked out?

"Someone," Davy said, and his voice was hard and clipped, not the usual soft drawl, "shot an' killed a heifer of mine out in th' back pasture last night. Butchered it right there and left th' blood an' guts scattered all over. Must've expected th' snow to last longer an' I wouldn't find it for awhile. Anyhow, th' snow did cover his tracks so there's not a trace to tell me who done it."

He was looking at me while he spoke, and his eyes narrowed and grew sharp. I swallowed and dragged my eyes away feeling slightly faint. The room seemed terribly hot after the cooler air outside. I turned my back and began to unbutton my coat.

"Me an' ol' Blue'll find 'im," Mr. Hilton said grimly. He was sitting by the fire cleaning his gun, and significantly, he raised the gun to his shoulder and squinted along the sights. I shivered.

"You stay out of it, Dad," said Davy, his voice quiet, almost deadly. "It was my heifer. I'll take care of it myself."

"An' let 'im go scott free, I s'pose," sneered his father.

Mr. Hilton leaned forward and propped his gun against the wall. He rose, pipe in hand, and went on into the living room. Clemmy turned back to whatever she'd been doing at the table. I went into my room and hung up my coat and in that moment felt a big hand on my shoulder, gripping and turning me. Another hand came up under my chin and lifted my face so that I was forced to look up into Davy's hard eyes.

"You know somethin'," he stated, in a flat low voice.

I didn't answer.

"Don't you think you oughta tell me?"

I pulled my chin away and bit my lip. "You—you're not supposed to be in my room," I stammered. He just stood there and looked at me. Presently I was forced to return his look.

"Davy, poverty does terrible things to people sometimes. I've seen it in the city. People who would ordinarily be decent, law-abiding citizens will sometimes do terrible things when they're hungry, or their families are in need, and—and an animal is not as important as people, as children are."

He didn't move, his expression didn't change.

"Children need to eat," I said desperately, twisting my hands in front of me. "They can't go on week after week—"

I stopped. It was no use, I would have to tell him. I let my hands fall to my sides and felt my shoulders slump a little.

"The little Proctor girls," I said quietly. "Their father drove them in today. He does sometimes. They haven't had anything for lunch except biscuits for weeks, your mother has been letting me take extra food for them. Today they had sandwiches, they showed me. Big chunks of beef between the biscuits."

Davy turned toward the door immediately, but I moved

quickly and blocked him.

"Davy, I don't know anything for sure," I said urgently, just above a whisper, my hands on his arms. "It doesn't have to mean he did it. There could have been some other way they got the meat. Davy, you have so much and they have so little."

He put me aside, almost gently. I followed him into the kitchen. He was putting his coat on.

"Davy," I said, my voice pleading.

He paused, his hand on the doorknob, and looked at me.

"Be careful," was all I said then and he was gone.

He wasn't back by suppertime. We ate without him. Clemmy and Mr. Hilton seemed unperturbed, but I was a bundle of nerves and could hardly eat, glancing often at the door. After they went to bed, I literally walked the floor, between times I stopped to peer out the window. At about nine o'clock, a light appeared in the shop window. I threw my coat across my shoulders and ran out, slipping and sliding in the mud, not thinking about boots until it was too late. I knocked and he opened the door and stood looking down at me.

"Davy, I was worried," I said breathing fast from my exertions. "Is—everything—all right?"

"I haven't shot anyone if that's what you're askin'. Not yet anyway."

"May I come in for a minute?"

He held the door wider and stood aside. I entered and slipped my shoes off at the door.

"Your feet'll freeze," he said.

"I got my shoes all muddy. I'll just stand on this rug. Davy, what happened? I've been so worried all evening. Maybe you'll think it's none of my business, but I—I can't just sit back, not knowing. Did you go to the Proctor's?"

"Yes."

"And did you find out anything? Oh, for Pete's sake, tell

me! I was the one who led you to believe he might have done it and he might be a completely innocent man."

"He done it all right."

"He did it," I corrected automatically, falling back into my role as teacher.

"Huh?"

"Oh, never mind, you say he did it?"

"Yeah."

"How do you know? Did he say so? Davy, please, I'm concerned about the girls."

He took the coat off my shoulders and pulled a chair over to me. I sat down and waited. He sat on the edge of his workbench.

"He answered th' door," Davy said slowly. "I asked him to step outside an' he reached back an' got his coat an' came on out. His wife said somethin', I don't know what, but I could see her an' she looked scared. Th' girls were there too. Anyhow, we went around th' house an' I jist asked him straight out what he knew about my heifer that was shot an' butchered out in my back pasture. He stood there for a minute, then he jist looked at me an' said, 'I done it.' I asked him why an' he said his family was hungry. I said what's wrong with th' rabbits an' squirrels an' possum in this section of th' hills an' he said he couldn't hit th' broad side of a barn with a gun. Don't know nothin' 'bout trappin' or huntin', I guess. He had a job at th' sawmill but lost it when they found some money missin'. He'd been in jail an' they accused him an' fired him. That's why they came out from th' city, to sort of get away from things, I guess, gossip an' all."

"Oh, Davy, how sad."

"I asked him if he stole the money, an' he said no. I asked him what he'd been in jail for an' he said armed robbery. Then I asked him if he done that an' he said no. Funniest thing, didn't volunteer anything at all hisself, but answered ever' question I asked him, quick an' quiet-like an' sort of hopeless. I went there mad as hops, intendin' to beat him to a pulp an' ended up feelin' sorry for him an' almost likin' him."

"Oh, Davy, I'm glad."

"But that don't bring my heifer back," he said gloomily.

"What did you decide to do?"

"I asked him what he thought I oughta do, an' he said he figgered Dad would either blow his head off, or I'd have him put back in jail. Said either way his family'd be better off, at least they'd have food to eat, th' state would have to see to that. They've been tryin' to live off nothin' for weeks, I guess. Never seen such a bare place."

"Did you go inside?"

"Yes, I went in an' met his wife an' th' girls."

"How did you come to do that?"

"Nosy, ain't you?" said Davy with the first sign of a grin I'd seen that evening.

"Yes, I'm dying of curiosity. Tell me every little detail."

"I told him he'd have to pay me for the cow an' he said he didn't have a nickel. Long an' short of it is, he's gonna work for me to pay it off. Don't know what he can do, bein' from th' city, I'll prob'ly have to teach him everything, but maybe he can chop wood or fix fence or somethin'. Might take awhile, 'cause I'll have to supply them with feed for th' mules, an' they'll have to have some other things for theirselves too."

"Davy, you are wonderful," I said softly. "I've been suspecting it for some time and now I know it for sure. I'm happy to claim you for a friend."

He was embarrassed and looked down at his hands. "I shoulda done somethin' for them before it come to this," he said slowly. "You told me how poor they was an' th' girls had nothin' to eat, but I forgot all about it, had other things on my mind."

"Don't blame yourself, Davy. It was my fault too. I should

have gone to visit them, found out more about their situation. For that matter, he should have come to you and asked you for work, I know you wouldn't have turned him down. But I suppose when you're in that position, it's difficult not to feel the whole world is against you. Anyhow, I'm glad it's turned out this way, and I'm very, very glad you're the kind of person you are, Davy."

I got up and put my coat on, and bent to my shoes. I happened to glance up just as he passed his hand wearily over his face. It must have been a difficult evening for him, I thought with quick sympathy. I straightened and went over to him and stood on tiptoe and kissed him on the cheek.

"Good night, friend," I said softly.

I had turned away when his hands reached out and pulled me back to him. He held me tight for a minute, his cheek against the top of my head. Then he said a rather gruff good night and let me go. I went back to the business of putting my muddy shoes on, keeping my head bent, knowing my color was high.

"He's lonely too," I thought with sudden clarity, "as lonely as I am, and just about as isolated. I don't think I ought to come out here again."

I gave him a brief smile as I went out the door. "Good night," I said again, and ran back to the cabin.

CHAPTER TWENTY-THREE

Target Practice

Mr. Proctor brought the girls to school again, then drove on toward the Hilton's. I was relieved. I'd been afraid perhaps he wouldn't keep his side of the bargain. After school he was there waiting for the girls. I would have liked to go out and speak to him, but didn't, because I felt unsure of what to say.

I saw very little of Davy in the next few days, he was busy in the evenings in his shop. The business of his slaughtered heifer was never mentioned again in my presence. I couldn't help wondering what he'd told his parents, if they realized the man who had done it was now working for Davy.

Friday after school, I decided to go out to the barn and have another look at the kittens. I was inside the center enclosure when I heard voices. It was Davy and another man, a voice I didn't recognize. It must be Mr. Proctor, he hadn't picked the girls up after school today. The men were somewhere behind the barn. My foot was on the bottom step leading to the hayloft when I heard the nearby boom of a gun.

I gasped and whirled around and ran outside and around the barn, terrified at what I might see. The two of them were standing close together. Davy was holding the gun and pointing. I stopped and clung to the side of the barn for a minute, breathless and faint with relief. They heard me and turned. Davy strode rapidly over to me.

"What's wrong?" he demanded.

I shook my head and moistened my lips. It took a real effort to push myself away from the support of the barn.

"Nothing," I said faintly. "You—you scared me. I didn't know there was anyone around with a gun."

"We were doin' some target practicin'," he said firmly, his eyes narrowed and compelling on mine.

I nodded. "So I see."

"Have you met Lewis Proctor? This is th' schoolteacher, Miss Davis."

I managed to smile and approach the man and hold out my hand. He took my hand briefly, his eyes met mine and looked away.

"I'm glad to meet you, Mr. Proctor. You have two very precious little girls. I'm enjoying having them in my school," I said in a more normal voice.

He was a smaller man than Davy and dressed poorly, but he was cleanshaven and neat. His face and demeanor were somber and almost shamed. He had to know by my mad rush around the barn what I had been afraid of, therefore that I knew about his crime. I felt sure Davy was going to be very angry with me.

"What is your target?" I asked to break the rather tense silence.

"That fence post there," Davy answered. "Wanna try it?"

I shuddered. "No. I don't like guns. I was on my way to see the kittens."

"They're not there."

"Where are they? You didn't drown them?"

"She moved them. Mother cats do that, you know. They don't like people handlin' their babies much when they're that little."

"Oh."

"Was you goin' into town tomorrow, Miss Davis?" he asked, and I glanced up at him, surprised. He hadn't called me Miss Davis for a long time.

"I thought I might, if the roads are all right."

"They're passable, I think. I was wonderin' if you'd be able to take Lewis's wife an' kids in with you? They're needin' to do some shoppin' an' he's gonna work on Jim's house with me tomorrow. He could bring them in this far an' then take them on back with him later."

"Of course, I'd be glad to have some company."

"Okay?" he asked of the other man, who nodded.

" 'Bout nine o'clock then," Davy told me and turned away. He passed the gun to the other man and gave a few instructions. I went back around the barn and headed toward the house, my feelings in something of a turmoil.

I heard the report of the gun several more times, then a short time later, the sound of the mules and wagon driving away. Davy came in and stood looking at me, hands on his hips. I was alone in the kitchen at the moment.

"I'm sorry," I said in a small voice.

"Great snakes, woman, did ya think if I was gonna take a shot at him I'd do it behind my own barn? That was what you was thinkin', wasn't it?"

"That, or he was taking a shot at you. Actually, I'm afraid I didn't think, I just heard the shot and panicked. I'd heard your voices a few minutes earlier, and—"

"An' what?"

"Nothing, I just panicked as I said."

"I told him what happened would jist be between him an' me. Think he believes that now?"

"Maybe he'll—he'll just believe I don't like guns and I was frightened. Well, what do you want me to do? I said I was sorry."

"Women," he snorted.

"Where would you be without us?"

I looked at him and he looked back. He pushed his much used hat to the back of his head and gave a gusty sigh.

"I'm sorry," I said again.

"S'all right. Forget it."

"Is it—going pretty well?"

"Better than I expected. He don't talk much but works good, if you show him what to do. I'll be glad of his help on Jim's house. That's too big a job for one man."

"I'm so glad. Doesn't it feel good to find someone who justifies your trust in him? So many times it doesn't work out that way."

He nodded. "I like him. He's smarter'n I am, got a high school education. Talks like you do, teacher."

"Then he didn't say, 'I done it,' " I said with a mischievous smile.

"What?"

"The other night you said when you asked him about the cow he said, 'I done it,' and I said 'He did it,' and you—oh never mind."

But he grinned at me. He knew what I was talking about.

"Doesn't mean he's smarter, Davy. There are different ways of being smart. Besides, you know how to use proper grammar, if you'd just get into the habit of it."

"Tryin' to reform me, teacher?"

"Would it do any good?"

"Might, you never can tell."

"About tomorrow," I reminded him. "Are the roads dried out?"

"Not entirely, but good enough if you're careful. I don't suppose you could drive th' truck?"

"No, and I'm certainly not going to try it on muddy roads or in city traffic."

"I can't take th' time or I'd go in tomorrow myself."

"Is it so urgent that they go in tomorrow?"

"Yes, they need things. I'm goin' ahead an' payin' him for this week's work so they can get a few things. He'll start payin' off th' heifer next week."

I smiled at him but didn't speak although his expression defied me to.

"Take her somewhere so she can get some sensible warm

clothes for th' girls an' herself, an' a few things like flour an' salt. No need to spend any of your money. I'll give them enough to get by on for now."

"Yes, Mr. Hilton," I said demurely.

"It ain't a good idea for them to get too much all at once."

"I believe I agree with you."

He eyed me doubtfully. "Mom sent a few things out already."

"I thought she would."

"I'll make sure you get out okay in th' morning."

"I'll be ready at nine, and I think it's a fine thing you're doing, Davy. If there's anything else I can do, let me know."

He nodded and left.

CHAPTER TWENTY-FOUR

A Davy Hat

Sue Proctor was quite an attractive young woman, but poverty and her husband's trouble had done devastating things to her. She seemed afraid to look directly at anyone, and barely mumbled a greeting when Davy introduced us. I stole a glance at her husband and saw the pain in his eyes as he looked at her.

I had the car warmed up and waiting when they arrived in the wagon. They were late and Davy helped her down, then the little girls and ushered them over to the car. He put her in front and the girls in the back, threw some tools in the back of the wagon and climbed up beside the other man.

"We'll follow you to th' turn off," he called to me. "We'll wait 'til you're through th' crick. You should be all right after that. If you have trouble, lay on th' horn an' we'll come pull you out."

I slid around a little but made it through all right. So far we had hardly exchanged a word. I thought she looked as if she'd been crying. The girls were quiet in the back seat.

"I'm glad I've finally got to meet you," I said when I was on the highway and could relax. "I've been trying to get around to visit all the parents of my children, but with the homes so far apart, it's been difficult. I met several at the pie supper, of course."

She made no comment, her eyes seemingly riveted on the view out the side window.

"Your girls are doing well in school, Mrs. Proctor. You've

taught them well at home. Those first three or four years are so important to a child's development. They are both going to be excellent readers, and as far as I'm concerned, that's half the battle in obtaining a good education."

I saw her swallow and blink rapidly, so I concentrated on my driving and was silent for the next several miles.

"Is there anywhere in particular you wanted to go?" I asked when we were nearing the outskirts of town. "What about a department store, 'Barber's' for instance? I go there sometimes."

She nodded and that was the end of conversation until I parked and we got out. I took the older girl, a second grader, by the hand and she took the younger one.

The first thing that caught my eye when we went in the store was a hat. There was a large sale display, and the most prominently featured hat was a wide-brimmed one of soft gray felt. It was a "Davy hat" if I ever saw one. We didn't stop, but my eyes kept going back to it. We went on to the children's department. She went straight to the blue jeans.

"I don't care if some people don't approve of jeans for girls," she said suddenly, a little defiantly. "My girls are going to be warm for a change."

"I think that's wise," I said casually. "They have quite a distance to come to school."

She picked out two pair of jeans each and two warm sweaters. I excused myself while she looked at socks and underclothes, and went back to the hat display.

"May I help you?" the salesman asked me.

"Could I see the gray hat, please?"

He took it down and handed it to me. I looked at the price tag and turned the hat around in my hands.

"I'm not sure of the size," I said. There was a mirror there and I stood before it and put the hat on my head. It came down over my eyes. The salesman and I both laughed as I removed it.

"Were you thinking of it for yourself, ma'am?" he asked doubtfully.

"No, for a friend. If I buy it and it doesn't fit, can I return or exchange it?"

"If you do it within a week while the sale is still on."

"All right. I'll take it."

I paid for it and took the sack and went back to Sue Proctor and her girls, wondering how foolish I'd been.

She was paying for two pair of socks and underclothes each for the girls, and counting the money left, an anxious look on her face.

"I want to look at shoes for the girls and a flannel shirt for Lewis, then I'm ready," she told me.

I saw that shoes for the girls cost more than she had expected, but she paid for them and we went to the men's department and looked at flannel shirts. We even giggled a little over some of the gaudy colors. She bought a red one because it was cheap but warm.

"Let's have some lunch," I said then. "I don't have much to buy today, so I'd like to treat you. There's a nice little family restaurant just around the corner here. Let's go there, then I need to get a few groceries for Clemmy before we go home."

I ordered a big lunch so she would feel free to do the same for herself and the girls. We talked a little then, and much more on the way home. She bought a few things at the grocery store and used all the money she had left. I was very tempted to slip her a few dollars, but remembered Davy's instructions and refrained.

"Do you know Davy Hilton very well?" she asked in a rather shy voice when we were out on the highway again.

"I've gotten fairly well acquainted with him since I started teaching here."

"He's a nice person, isn't he?"

"Very nice."

"He's been so kind."

"He's a kind person."

"Lewis said—he said he thought you knew about—" She hesitated and stopped.

"Yes," I said gently. "I've been very concerned about the girls and I suspected—anyhow, I asked Davy and he told me, but I promise you it won't go any further."

"Miss Davis, Lewis never did anything like that before, I swear to you. He was desperate and so worried about the girls. We both were." She glanced over the back seat at the girls. "You can't understand what it's like to be so terribly poor."

"I know. I mean I've never been in that position, but I can understand your concern for the girls."

"I appreciated the coats you gave them and the lunches, but—"

"Clemmy and Ellen sent the coats and Clemmy actually provided the lunches," I broke in.

"It must have seemed terribly ungrateful when—" She stopped again, her voice choked. "I didn't know he was going to do it, but he told me afterwards. I was so afraid and when Davy came—Lewis cried after he left. I've never seen him cry before, not even when he was sent to jail for something he didn't do, but he cried and cried that night, and since then he's been a little more hopeful. He says Davy is going to keep him on even after he pays for the heifer, so Lewis will be able to have a steady job again. You don't know what that means to him and to me, Miss Davis."

"I think that's wonderful. I'd like for you to call me Anne, please. After all, we're about the same age."

"I expect I'm a little older than you. I know I feel a hundred sometimes, but if this works out—"

"It's going to work out, Davy will keep his promise. He's that kind of person."

"Sometime, in a few weeks," she said a little hesitant, maybe you and he would come out some evening? It gets so terribly lonely out there and—and we don't have any friends."

I had reached the turn off into the muddy road and hoped she put down my hesitance to preoccupation with my driving. "I'd like that," I said then. "And maybe someday you'd like to come in with your husband and spend the day or at least part of the day at school. That's permissible you know, in fact, I like for parents to do that occasionally. It shows the child that the parents are interested in his or her education."

"I will someday when I get some different clothes."

We didn't talk much more. When we pulled up at the cabin, it was mid-afternoon. There was no sign of the men so the four of us went inside. Clemmy was alone. I introduced her and her manner was as kind and hospitable as always.

"You'll stay to supper," she said. "Th' men won't be home 'fore then."

"Thank you. If you're sure—"

"There's plenty," Clemmy said. She brought out a few toys for the girls. I took my package to my room and hid it under the bed. Then I invited Sue in. The room was warm enough. Clemmy always kept my door open during the day. I left the door ajar, invited Sue to sit on the rocker, sat on the edge of the bed myself, and lowered my voice.

"I have an idea," I said. "I have some jeans that I can't wear here. Clemmy and Mr. Hilton don't approve of them for women, so naturally I don't want to offend them. Last time I tried on a pair they had either shrunk or I've put on weight, the latter, I suspect. Clemmy is such a good cook. If you can wear them you can have them. Why don't you try them on?"

Her lip quivered and I rose and turned my back to take the

143

jeans out of my suitcase where I still had them packed away. I took a sweater off its hanger and a longsleeved blouse and laid the four garments across the bed."

"See if they fit. I'll be back in a minute."

I went out, closing the door behind me. Clemmy was starting preparation for supper.

"I'll be back to help you in a little while, Clemmy," I said.

"You don't have company much, why don't you jist visit some? They's plenty of time."

When I went back into the bedroom, Sue had on a pair of the jeans and the sweater. She was so thin, they rather hung on her, but they would pass. She was looking in the mirror, running a hand through her hair.

"You look nice," I said. "My word, I'd better go on a diet. They positively bulged at the seams when I put them on."

"I'm thin, but I'll fill out soon. You have a beautiful shape, you're not fat. Did you—really mean for me to have these?"

"Yes, I can't use the jeans here, and I have plenty of blouses and sweaters."

"Thank you, you're so kind. I hope someday maybe I can do something for you."

"Maybe you can."

"I didn't know there was such kindness in the world anymore. You don't know what it's like—"

"Sue, there's a lot of kindness left in the world. Generally people are willing to help if they're just aware of the need, or know how to go about it. I'm sorry I didn't do something before. I knew you needed help, but I just didn't know how to go about it. Let me help now. If there's anything else you need and I have it, I'm willing to share with you."

"No, there's nothing else, we'll get by now, except—"

"Except?"

"You've done so much, I hate to ask, but—my hair. It

used to be bright and shiny, Lewis always said it looked like sunshine in the morning, but I've had to wash it lately with hand soap and it's so dull and drab."

"I have plenty of shampoo. I bought a new bottle last week and haven't opened it yet. Let me wash and set it for you. I used to do my sister's hair. Clemmy won't mind."

"Can I wear these here?"

"Oh, no, I wouldn't. I'll loan you a skirt."

Clemmy didn't get any help with supper at all that afternoon. Sue and I washed each other's hair, then partially dried it before the fire before we set it in big rollers. I got out my cold cream and makeup and we experimented for all the world like two teenagers. I enjoyed the afternoon and her eyes were sparkling by the time the men came in for supper. Her hair was soft and shining when we took the curlers out and brushed it. I looked in the mirror at my brown curls and felt almost jealous. She was very attractive.

Her husband stopped just inside the door and stared at her. Davy stared too. She stood, her smile a little tremulous, her hands gripped together in front of her.

"We—I—Anne washed my hair and set it this afternoon," she stammered.

"And she washed my hair and set it," I said.

"Nice," Davy said. "Mom, this is Sue's husband, Lewis."

Supper was a rather quiet affair. Mr. Hilton didn't come in, he must have been off on one of his frequent hunting trips, and I thought it was probably just as well.

Lewis had almost nothing to say but he kept glancing over at his wife. When the meal was over, he said they had to go, and Sue went into my room and changed back into her own dress. I put the jeans and blouses in a grocery bag for her and slipped in the shampoo. Davy and I saw them off. At the last minute, Sue ran back and put her arms around me and hugged me. She threw a slight smile and a breathless 'thank you' at Davy and ran back to the wagon.

"Must've gone okay," Davy observed to me when they had driven away.

"I think it did. She's terribly lonely, poor girl."

"Didn't know she was that pretty."

"She likes you too," I said demurely. "Couldn't praise you enough."

He looked at me, startled and then uneasy.

"Don't worry, Davy," I said with a little laugh. "She's crazy about her husband, but things have been hard, and right now she's got a bad case of hero worship. It'll pass." When he didn't speak, I continued thoughtfully. "If you like, I can tell her how disagreeable and hard to get along with you can be, and how bossy."

He took his hat off and swung at me with it. I dodged but reached out and grabbed the hat.

"Can I see your hat a minute, Davy?"

"What for?" he asked, running his hand through his hair, but he let go of it. I put it on my head and it slipped down over my eyes. I felt better and handed it back to him.

"What was that for?"

"Oh, nothing."

"Thinkin' of swipin' my hat or somethin'? It's th' only one I got. Had it for years."

"I can tell," I said drily.

"If you don't like it, what you tryin' to swipe it for?"

"I wasn't. Are you going out to your shop now?"

"Yep. Why?"

"Would you come in a minute later this evening? There's something I'd like to discuss with you."

"About the Proctors?"

"Yes, about the Proctors."

"Okay. See ya later."

He came in about nine o'clock. I was reading beside the kitchen stove. He hung his coat and hat on a nail and pulled up the other chair and sat down beside me.

"Well, teacher?" he asked. "What's th' problem?"

"No problem."

"Didn't run up a bunch of bills all over town, by any chance?"

"Of course not. I just took her to the store and she picked out what she wanted."

"Did she get what she needed?"

"For the girls she did. One shirt for Lewis, but nothing for herself."

"What was that sack she carried out of your room?"

"Nosy. I gave her two pair of jeans, a sweater and a blouse. I don't need them here."

"An' you didn't spend any of your money on her?"

"Not on her. Oh, I bought lunch for them, was that okay, boss?"

"I reckon. Well?"

"I just thought—you'd like to know how grateful they both are. She said—she said he cried after you left that first night, and he's beginning to feel hopeful again and that you've offered him a permanent job."

"He's a good worker, I can use him."

He waited, looking at me. I closed my book and bit my lip.

"Was that it?"

"No."

"Then?"

"Oh, nuts," I said. I got up and took the sack from under my bed and brought it back with me.

"I bought you a present," I said, holding it out.

He was surprised and didn't look at all pleased. "What is it?" he asked.

"Open it and see."

He slowly opened the sack and took out the hat. He sat a long time with it in his hand, looking down at it, before he lifted his eyes to me.

"I didn't know the size," I said. "I hope it fits."

"I told you not to spend your money on them, so you spend it on me instead?"

"It wasn't—I didn't intend to, it just kind of jumped out at me. It just—somehow looked like you, so I bought it. The man said if it doesn't fit, you can exchange it, if you do it in a week. It was on sale."

He was looking back down at the hat, turning it around slowly in his hands.

"Don't you like it?"

"Always wanted a hat like this," he said gruffly.

"Then try it on."

He rose and stood before the small mirror above the washstand and put it carefully on his head. I clasped my hands in delight.

"I knew it would suit you and it does. The minute I saw it I thought, 'that's a Davy hat,' and it is. I'm glad I bought it. You look like the hero in a Wild West movie."

He had turned and was looking at me. "You shouldn't've, teacher."

"Yes, I should. It's definitely your hat. Besides, you and your mother do so much for me, and I wanted to buy it."

"Then thanks," he said and bent and kissed me on the cheek.

CHAPTER TWENTY-FIVE

Clemmy's Home Remedy

I saw very little of Davy all that next week. He and Lewis Proctor were working on Jim's house during the day, and Davy worked in his shop evenings, filling an order for cabinets from his brother John. I missed Davy, simply because it meant I spent the long evening hours completely alone. But I had my homework to do, and I'd always been an avid reader, so I managed fairly well.

On Friday morning I woke with a tickling, scratchy throat, and feeling of depression. I went on to school, wondering vaguely if I was coming down with something. Some of the children had colds and coughs and runny noses, there had been several cases of absenteeism.

A few minutes before school was to begin, Lewis Proctor drove into the schoolyard with his children, and Sue jumped down and came in with the girls. She was bright-eyed and smiling as she greeted me.

"Sue!" I exclaimed with genuine pleasure. "Did you come to visit with us today?"

"No, I just stopped to say hello," she said. "Lewis is waiting for me. I'm going on to the house where they're working. Davy said they need some cleaning up done, sawdust and shavings and bits and pieces of boards, and he said I could do it and he's going to pay me. Isn't it wonderful? I get out of that house for a whole day to be around people, and get paid for it besides. Maybe I can get myself a dress with the money, then I'll be able to come and visit school. Well, I've got to go. Lewis said I could only stay a minute, but I wanted to see you and thank you again for all you've done."

She ran back out and got in the wagon, waving to me as they drove away. Strangely, I felt even more depressed after she left, and I was puzzled by it. Surely I was glad to see her looking well and so much happier. I put it down to the cold that I was positive I was getting now.

By the end of the day my head felt stuffed up, my throat hurt, I had a headache and was running a fever. Thank goodness it was Friday. Maybe if I went right to bed when I got back to the cabin, I'd be better by Monday.

When I stepped into the kitchen, Clemmy took one look at me, dropped her mending, and rose and took my books.

"I thought this mornin' you looked peaked," she said. "You get undressed an' get right to bed. You're burnin' up, child."

She helped me off with my coat and hustled me toward my room. My teeth began to chatter together as she helped me undress. I got into my flannel nightgown and under the covers, and Clemmy left me. A minute later she was back, and bending over me, smeared a strong-smelling salve on my throat and upper chest and put a warmed flannel cloth over the salve before she rebuttoned my gown. It burned my skin and the smell nearly strangled me for the first few minutes.

I drifted off to sleep, dozing off and on for the rest of the afternoon. I was vaguely aware of the muted sounds of Davy and his father coming in for supper, then going out again. Clemmy had left my door ajar for warmth. Twice she came in with a glass of fresh water and made me drink it all. Before she went to bed she gave me two aspirin and again rubbed the offensive-smelling salve on my throat and chest.

I slept again but restlessly, and woke with a moan on my lips and a rough hand brushing the hair back from my forehead. I turned my head and saw in the dim lamplight from the kitchen that Davy was sitting on the edge of my bed.

"What're you doing here?" I croaked fretfully.

"Told Mom I'd check on you when I came in to build up th' fire," he answered. "Feeling pretty rotten?"

"If you must know, yes," I answered irritably.

"Mad at me?"

"I'm sorry."

"Mom said you should drink lots of water. I brought in some fresh."

"You didn't have to do that."

"But I did. Drink it up like a good girl."

He took the glass from the desk and held it out to me. I struggled to a sitting position and took it.

"Still got plenty of ointment on?"

"Can't you tell? I must reek to high heaven."

"Don't want me to put more on for you?"

"No, thanks. What in the world is it, anyhow?"

"Mom makes it. It's got turpentine, an' lard, an' kerosene, besides a few other things in it. Skunk oil, maybe."

"Ugh. That would explain the smell all right."

"You'll be red as a beet tomorrow, but it works. How's th' head?"

"Still there."

"Yep, so it is. Th' fever too, your cheeks are red. Anything else I can do?"

"Don't bring me any more water," I said irritably. "Now I have to go to the bathroom."

"'Fraid I can't do that for you," he said rising. "Use th' pot."

"I can't."

"You can too. You're not goin' outside tonight."

He went out, pulling the door shut behind him. I threw the covers back and got out of bed. I went over and hooked the door, bent down and pulled the covered enamel pot out from under the bed and looked distastefully at it.

When I had unhooked the door and pulled it ajar and got back in bed, my teeth were chattering again. I huddled down under the covers and felt miserable and sorry for myself, and felt tears begin to gather behind my eyes.

Davy came back in carrying a steaming cup which he put on the desk. He bent and slid his arm under me and lifted me up so that I was again in a half-sitting position against the pillows. I wiped my sleeve across my eyes and tried not to sniff.

"What's th' matter?" he asked. "Got th' blues?"

"I think—I must be a little homesick."

He sat down again on the side of my bed and it gave under his weight so that I tilted sideways. He reached out and lifted and straightened me as if I'd been a child, then handed me the cup. It smelled of liquor.

"What is it?" I asked.

"Not poison, jist lemon an' honey an' whiskey."

"Whiskey?"

"Not enough to make you drunk, jist enough to warm you an' soothe your throat. Take a sip."

I did, cautiously, and felt the warmth seep down into my body. It was strong but not unpleasant and it did soothe my throat. I took another sip.

"Not too fast, a little at a time. Does that help?"

"Yes, it does, thanks," I said and added, self-conscious at his nearness, "I must reek of that ointment."

"Add to that whiskey breath," he said, grinning at me. "You may have to take a bath in Mom's ol' washtub yet, but at least you'll probably get to have your own water, bein' th' teacher an' all."

"My own water?"

"Um-huh. There was nine of us kids, you know, so when we took a bath in th' washtub, we all used th' same water.

Saved all that carryin' an' heatin' of water, you know."

"You're not serious? All nine of you in the same water?"

"Actually, wasn't quite that bad. Th' five boys bathed on Saturday night an' th' four girls an' Mom on Sunday night."

"And you had one tub of water each time?"

"Yep. Course when we got older if we wanted our own private bath, we could, but we had to carry in our own wood an' water an' empty th' tub after. For awhile there, seemed like someone was always takin' a bath, mostly th' girls. We younger ones would get run out of th' kitchen an' sometimes we'd bang on th' doors or try to peek through th' windows. Had more fights over that."

"Sounds like something you'd do," I said, amused, aware of a desire to keep him talking. "What about your father? When did he take his bath?"

He scratched his head. "Dunno," he said. "Never knew him to take a bath, 'cept in summer. Then we all went into th' crick whenever we wanted to."

"Did you have a good childhood, Davy? Were you happy?"

"Dunno, never thought much about it, I guess. Don't remember feelin' 'specially deprived. Always had food an' plenty to do. Are you finished with that?"

"Yes, thank you, that did help. I feel warm and sleepy now."

I slid down into the bed and he bent over and tucked the covers in around my shoulders.

"Holler if you need me," he said rising.

"I'm okay, really. Please don't stay in because of me." I heard my voice taper off, saw Davy go through the door, then saw and heard no more until morning.

I stayed in bed all the next day and Clemmy kept me smeared with the salve and saw that I drank a full glass of water every hour or so it seemed. I dozed off and on and by afternoon started to feel better. I sat up and prepared a test for my eighth graders to be given on Monday, and did a little reading. I saw nothing of the rest of the family although I heard them coming and going through my half-open door. Before she went to bed that night Clemmy brought in more warm lemon and honey and whiskey and said Davy said to sip on it before I went to sleep. I did, and slept well that night and woke feeling very much better.

My fever and headache were gone, though my throat was still a little sore. Clemmy brought me breakfast in bed, bacon and eggs and biscuits and I was able to eat most of it.

"Clemmy," I said, "your ointment has done wonders for me, but I'd like to wash it off now. Would that be all right?"

"You might oughta keep it on an' stay in bed today."

"I can't stand this bed a minute longer and I certainly can't be around anyone smelling as I do. Please, Clemmy, I'll be good and take a nap this afternoon."

I smiled winningly at her and she smiled back. "Davy said you might be wantin' a bath in th' tub," she said.

I considered it. Well, why not? It would be more effective than a washcloth at least, and it would be another experience to tell my grandchildren.

"I would, Clemmy, if it's not too much trouble."

"I'll have Davy bring in more water."

I stayed in my room and heard Davy coming and going in the kitchen. I got up and unbuttoned the neck of my nightgown before the mirror. My skin was so red I looked as if I'd gotten a bad sunburn. I washed my neck and upper chest with a washcloth, but didn't get rid of the smell. I put on my bathrobe and went into the kitchen. The stove was covered with pans of hot water, the washtub on the floor behind the stove. Clemmy was bringing out towels and a washcloth.

She drew the curtains across the windows, locked the outside door, and went into the living room. I assumed the men had gone for the day but went over and hooked the living room door just in case.

I got out clean underwear, shampoo and soap, then went back and viewed my bath. The washtub was almost half full of water, with a bucket of warm water and a dipper on the washstand for rinsing. Feeling wryly amused, I got out of my clothes and stepped into the tub.

I tried to sit down, but couldn't. Then I tried getting down on my knees but my legs were too cramped. I sat down with my legs hanging over the edge, but that didn't last long either, it was too awkward and uncomfortable. I ended up squatting in the tub, soaping myself thoroughly, then dipping water up to rinse myself. I had almost finished and was standing, carefully pouring dipperfuls of water over my shoulders, when the doorknob into the living room rattled vigorously and there was a loud knock on the door. I gave a start and spilled water on the floor.

"Hey, let me in," demanded Davy's voice. "What you got th' door locked for?"

I had to smile, remembering what he'd told me about bath time when he was a boy. He was teasing me and I could hear it in his voice.

"I need my hat," he said plaintively. "Open th' door."

I giggled. "Just for that, Davy Hilton, you'll have to wait until I wash my hair too."

I stepped out of the tub and dried myself and put on my underclothes and bathrobe. Then on my knees I bent and shampooed my hair, again rinsing with dippers of warm water. I took my time, then with a towel around my head, went and unhooked the door into the living room and pushed it open. Davy rose from his chair and came in.

"Manage okay?" he asked with a sardonic grin.

"I managed fine, thank you." I sat down near the stove and began combing out my wet hair.

"You look like a drowned rat."

"Thanks. Thought you needed your hat."

"Forgot I had it on all th' time. Do that sometimes, it's real soft and comfortable, you know."

"I believe you, of course."

He stood, grinning at me, his hands hooked in his pockets. "How have th' mighty fallen," he said softly. "First Mom's skunk ointment, then th' pot, an' now a bath in th' washtub. What's this world comin' to, anyway?"

"Don't you have work to do?" I asked frigidly. I made the mistake of looking up at him, and felt my lips twitch. I laughed. "I'm storing it all up to tell my grandchildren," I said.

"Good idea, Grandma. Glad you're better. Be seein' you."

"Thanks for bringing all that water in."

"Okay."

He reached out and tweaked my hair. "Don't try to empty th' tub. I'll do that later."

"Thanks."

CHAPTER TWENTY-SIX

A Girl Like You

Someone was calling my name but I couldn't answer. I was fathoms deep in sleep and was finding it very difficult to surface. When I did open my eyes, it was to see Davy's face above me, to feel his hands on my shoulders. I must have looked alarmed because one of his hands came over immediately and covered my mouth.

"Sh-h," he whispered. "It's all right, I need your help. Calvin needs your help."

He removed his hands and I sat up. Calvin stood in shadows at the side of my room. I threw the cover back and went to him.

"What is it, Calvin?" I asked, kneeling beside him and putting my arms across his shoulders. His words came in a rush, barely audible.

"There was a bobcat got in th' pigpen last night. We woke up 'cause th' pigs was squealin' and th' dog barkin'. Granny got th' gun an' we went out an' saw him with th' pig in his mouth. Granny shot him but he got away. He was lame, but he got away 'fore Granny could reload. She made me wait 'til it got light, then said for me to run an' get Davy, so I did."

"What a brave boy you are, Calvin," I said.

"A injured bobcat is dangerous, Anne," Davy broke in, also speaking in little more than a whisper. "He has to be found 'fore th' kids start to school. That's why I've got to

157

have Dad's help. He's a better tracker, better hunter than I am, knows cats better too. I'm gonna get him up now, but I want you to keep Cal with you. Don't let him leave 'til we come back with th' cat, and don't you leave th' house either."

He was gone, pulling my door shut behind him. I knelt there beside Calvin, neither of us speaking, but listening to the sounds in the next room.

When I was sure Davy and his father were gone, I opened the door and peeked out. Clemmy was building up the fire, her hair untidy around her face. Should I bring Calvin out now or keep him in my room?

"Do you want to sleep awhile in my bed?" I whispered to him. "You must be tired."

He shook his head. I made up my mind and opened my door, drawing Calvin with me. Clemmy glanced up, a look of surprise crossed her face and was quickly gone. I explained the situation to her.

"I'll start breakfast," was all she said. "You'll be hungry after bein' up half th' night, Calvin. If you want to get dressed, th' boy can stay here with me."

I took the teakettle to my room and poured water in my wash pan and returned it to the kitchen. I dressed in a warm sweater and skirt and my sensible shoes. We had breakfast and sat around and waited. It was over an hour and the men were not back yet. I was getting quite nervous, some of the children would be starting for school before too much longer.

Calvin was at the window, his nose squashed, his hands crumpling the curtains. "They're comin'," he said in sudden excitement. "They got him."

I went to the window and looked. The two men were coming over the hill, Davy carrying the guns, the animal thrown over Mr. Hilton's shoulder. I wondered what to do about Calvin. Davy had said for me to keep him with me, but did he want his father to find him in the house? Calvin solved the problem for me by turning and slipping into the living room and out the front door. Clemmy was putting our three used plates into the dishwater. I felt faintly resentful on behalf of Calvin, but I slipped my coat on and went outside to meet them. I was curious about the bobcat, picturing in my mind something between a house cat and a tiger.

Mr. Hilton swung the cat down and stood him on his feet in a lifelike position. I took an involuntary step backward. The cat had died with a snarl, his lips drawn back over long sharp teeth.

"He's a big 'un," Mr. Hilton said with satisfaction. "See that front leg? Been hurt sometime, caught in a trap likely. Couldn't hunt proper with that lame leg, that's what drove him to try th' pigpen. They don't come in that close anymore, 'cept they're desprit. Ever seen one?"

"No, and I'm glad. I hope I never meet up with a live one. Is that why they call it a bobcat, because of its short tail?"

"Yup, that's why."

He heaved it up on his shoulders again and went off toward the barn. I looked up at Davy.

"Cal gone?" he asked.

"Yes, he slipped out when he saw you coming."

"You on your way too?"

"Just about."

"Wait an' I'll come with you. Didn't get a chance to build up th' fire this mornin'."

"Your mother is getting your breakfast. I can build the fire, Davy, you don't always have to do it."

"Don't mind. I'll jist put these guns inside an' clean them later."

"Go ahead and eat your breakfast then, Davy. There's time. I'll wait."

I gathered up my books and papers and had another cup of coffee while Davy ate breakfast. When we left for school,

Mr. Hilton had still not come from the barn. Davy and I didn't seem to have much to say to each other.

"How are the Proctors doing?" I asked finally.

"Pretty good, I think."

"Is—Sue still working with you too?"

"Sue? Oh, no, she jist worked that one day. She comes with Lewis sometimes though. Gets lonesome by herself, I guess. Picks up a little and hands us things, you know, but mostly jist sets and watches."

"I see. Strange how friendships come about sometimes, isn't it?"

"Yep, sure is."

"The three of you are friends now, aren't you?"

"I think so. I like them, at least. Only one thing still botherin' me 'bout that deal."

"Your heifer?"

"Th' way he butchered her," he said. "You never saw anything like it. Wasted at least half th' meat. Gonna have to teach him how to butcher a cow right, I guess." He looked at me and grinned. "Not," he added, " 'til he gets his own cow though."

We had reached the schoolyard and he went off to the woodpile while I went on up and unlocked the door. It was strange to walk into a cold room. Always before it had been warm and inviting.

Davy started the fire and brought in more wood, while I went around straightening up the room. He primed the pump, then came in and adjusted the damper on the stove. He stopped before me on his way out, hat in hand, looking down at it as he turned it around and around.

"Nice hat you've got there, Mr. Hilton," I said lightly.

"Ain't it a beaut? Some of th' guys been tryin' to trade me out of it."

"What is it, Davy?"

He looked up at me then. "Wish I was better with words," he said.

"We've never had any trouble understanding one another, have we? Except right at first, of course. Is it about Calvin?"

"No. Jist wanted to tell you I think you're really somethin'."

"You do?"

"Yep. Th' way you treat these kids, 'specially Calvin, and th' help you gave Sue. She was like a different person when we come back that first day. An' 'specially th' way you treat Mom. Sometimes th' teachers, bein' from th' city, you know, don't fit in too good, an' they don't like th' hours we keep an all, but you've been different. You fit in here and you treat Mom special. You're good for her. Some of us, th' family, kinda take her for granted, I guess. An' there's th'—"

"Stop, Davy. I appreciate your compliments, but you'll be giving me the big head. I haven't done anything out of the ordinary, really, and as for your mother, it isn't hard to be nice to her, you know. She's a beautiful person. But thank you anyhow, Davy."

"That fella in St. Louis, Don somethin' or other, I hope he knows how lucky he is. Wish I could find myself a girl like you. I'd get married in a minute."

He put his hat on his head, adjusted it to the right angle, nodded to me and left. I sat there a moment musing over his words. Had he been serious? Sometimes it was hard to tell with Davy.

Well, he was a fine person and I liked him a lot, but there was no way my liking would go beyond friendship. I had my plans for the future all made and those plans didn't include anyone by the name of Davy Hilton.

CHAPTER TWENTY-SEVEN

Luther Gets Drunk

Davy was at the washstand shaving before the mirror. I was sitting at the kitchen table, papers spread out before me, but I kept glancing up at him, finding it difficult to concentrate.

He was going into town and I hadn't been in for several weeks. After my illness, the weather turned rainy and gusty, so I had been confined to the cabin on the weekends. Davy must know I was longing to go into town but he made no offer to take me along.

He must have a date, he didn't usually shave in the evenings and he'd asked his mother to iron a special shirt. I was curious and resentful. It wouldn't hurt him to let me come along, he could drop me off in town and pick me up later. I wouldn't interfere with his date. I wondered who the girl was, I'd not been aware of his dating anyone before. Of course, that didn't mean he didn't. I didn't often see him in the evenings these days. I caught his eyes on me in the mirror and dropped my own eyes quickly.

He splashed water over his face, dried, then patted on a good-smelling aftershave. He was going to a lot of trouble for her, whoever she was. He turned and stripped off his shirt and reached for the shirt his mother had ironed and draped over a chair. I worked industriously at my papers, but I was very aware of broad shoulders and rippling muscles and somehow knew his eyes were on me. He buttoned the shirt and pushed the tail down into his jeans. I was faintly embarrassed, wishing he wouldn't dress in front of me in that uninhibited way. He ran a belt through the loops in his jeans and fastened the rather ornate buckle, then sat down to pull on a pair of western boots.

"Sorry I can't take you with me, little one," he said gently then.

"Who wants you to?" I retorted.

"Not you?"

"Don't be silly."

"Okay."

He slipped into his jacket, put the hat I'd given him on his head, and paused with his hand on the doorknob.

"See you later."

"I hope you get stuck," I said with sudden venom. He was startled and so was I. I felt the color rising in my face, and closed my eyes in mortification. "I'm sorry. I didn't mean that."

"Damn it all," he said softly but distinctly before he jerked the door open and went out.

"Oh, great," I muttered to myself. "What in the world is the matter with me?"

"Did Davy leave?" Clemmy asked from the living room doorway.

"Yes, he did."

"I don't like to see him get mixed up with that girl."

I knew it wasn't my business, but I was curious. "What girl?"

"That Sutton girl. I think they call her Goldie or somethin' like that."

"I met her at the pie supper. He seemed quite interested in her then."

"I don't like it," she said again, rather heavily.

"I expect he can take care of himself."

She took herself off to bed and very soon after, I threw my pencil down, scraped the papers together and stuck them in the folder I carried. I put on my flannel gown and my bathrobe and crawled into bed with a new novel. The lamplight was dim, so I relit one of the kitchen lamps and put it on my desk. That was better and I relaxed and was soon engrossed in the novel.

At around eleven o'clock I was getting sleepy but I wanted to finish the story, so I got up and checked the coffeepot that was always on the back of the stove. There was some there, but it would be strong. I'd have to dilute it with milk. I put the lamp I was carrying on the table and reached up for a cup, just as the kitchen door burst open. I gasped and jumped back. Two men seemed to be struggling just outside the door.

"Quiet," said Davy's voice, short and rather breathless. "Don't wake Mom up. It's Luther. Can you help me get him inside?"

I went over and grasped Luther's other arm and pulled on him. Davy seemed to be pulling and lifting at the same time, and together we got him through the door and into a chair.

"Sorry," Davy said, out of breath. "Didn't want Mom to wake up an' see him like this."

"Is he sick?"

"Drunk. Is th' other door shut?"

"It's shut. What can I do? Bread? Coffee?"

"Coffee might help. He's chilled clear through. Found him layin' in th' middle of th' road, durn near run over him, would've if his mule hadn't stayed with him."

I poured a cup of the black coffee and Davy held it to his lips. His teeth chattered against the cup, he was shivering violently, and only took a sip or two.

"Gotta spit," he said suddenly, in a thick voice. He weaved his way over to the stove and took one of the covers off and spit. When he tried to replace the cover it clattered around the hole but never went in place. I took it from him, afraid the noise would wake the older Hiltons. Davy helped him back to the chair. I brought the top quilt from my bed and wrapped it around him.

"If he doesn't get pneumonia I'll be surprised," I said. "How long do you suppose he'd been lying out there?"

"Hours maybe. I oughta get him home but his mother will have a fit. She'll be worried sick as it is. Don't know what I oughta do."

"I think you'd better strip him and put him to bed in your old room. He's not fit to even be sitting up."

"I think maybe you're right. Come Luther."

He bent and put his hands under Luther's arms and heaved him up to his feet. As big and strong as Davy was, I could see it took a real effort to steer Luther in the right direction and keep him on his feet.

I ran ahead and pulled the covers back. "Are there any of your clothes left here?" I asked Davy. "His are quite damp."

"In th' dresser there."

I found a warm shirt and an old pair of jeans and laid them out on the bed. Davy was already stripping his shirt off. I left the room but as I left I heard Luther say something quite lucid, but didn't catch what it was, just my name, Miss Davis.

I put the quilt back on my bed and stirred up the fire. When Davy came back I knew he was worried.

"Is he asleep?"

"Will be in a minute."

"What did he say about me?"

"Said, 'don't tell Miss Davis I got drunk today.' "

I gave a little snort of laugh. "Well, that's something at least, that he should feel ashamed."

"Luther's not had a easy life, Anne. I hope—well, never mind. Maybe Dad was right, maybe some kids are better off workin' instead of going' to school."

"Luther's missed more school than he's attended for several weeks, so you may be right in this instance. Never saw anyone so resistant to learning."

"He's not a bad kid."

"Maybe not, but he's sure got a good start."

"S'pose I'd better go on out an' tell his mom he's here. She'll be worried. Would you mind keepin' a eye on him while I'm gone? He'll sleep, I think."

"All right."

He reached into his jacket pocket and fished out a package of gum and handed it to me.

"Brought you somethin'."

"Thanks." I reached out and took the gum almost reluctantly.

"Didn't get stuck, but didn't have much fun either. You didn't miss out on anything."

"Oh, I don't know about that," I said casually. "You've got lipstick all over the front of your jacket."

He glanced down and a slow flush spread over his face. He looked back up at me.

"Don't s'pose it'd do any good to tell you that was her idea, not mine."

"Why should I care one way or the other?" I asked coldly.

He turned to the door. "I'll be back as soon as I can."

I didn't answer. I was feeling vaguely ashamed of myself.

CHAPTER TWENTY-EIGHT

These Lonesome Hills

I was more lonely than I'd ever been in my life before. It was one thing to say I didn't mind my own company, quite another to actually have to put it to the test day after day after day in these lonesome hills.

The days grew shorter, the evenings longer. The elder Hiltons went to bed earlier and earlier, and Davy went out to his shop right after supper. Sometimes he came in late to build up the fires but I was always in bed by then. I thought of inventing a problem so I could go and consult with him about it, but what problem? I could tell him Luther hardly came to school at all lately, but I was sure he already knew that. I could say I was worried about Calvin, but in actual fact, Calvin was doing fine. So what other excuse could I use? I threw my pencil down and pushed my chair back. So my excuse would have to be a lame one. I couldn't stand this peace and quiet a minute longer. I threw my coat over my shoulders and ran outside.

I hesitated when I got to the shop. I could see Davy through the window bent over some work. He might not appreciate my interruption, but a person could take only so much of his own company.

It was a minute before he opened the door to my knock. He looked surprised and perhaps not too pleased.

"Could I talk to you a minute if you're not too busy?"

He held the door open and stood aside. The room was

rather crowded with the cabinets he was making and his various tools. There were shavings all over the floor.

" 'Fraid I'm in a mess here," he said.

"Would you like for me to clean it up for you?"

"No. I'd jist mess it up again."

I felt a little chagrined. Sue Proctor could clean up for him, but I couldn't, evidently.

"Are these the cabinets John ordered?"

"Yep."

"They're going to be very nice." I ran my hand along the wood, not looking at him, and felt I shouldn't have come. He went back to smoothing a long piece of wood with a hand plane. Thin curls fell away to the floor, he seemed to be fully occupied with the work he was doing.

"What's th' problem?" he asked, not looking up.

"Luther. is worrying me."

He did look up then and put the plane down. He propped himself against the table and picked at the shavings.

"He's been missing so much, Davy. He's only been to school one day this week and he wasn't in the best of moods then. I'm going to have no choice but to fail him again."

He didn't answer for a minute, he was frowning and thoughtful.

"I've been thinkin' I ought to maybe see if John'll take him on, give him a job, see if he can get a little trainin' in buildin' or brick layin'. I thought maybe when school is out, but if he's not goin', I might ought to go ahead with it now."

"He'll be sixteen in a few weeks, old enough to quit if he wants, and I think he will."

"If Brad'll let him."

"Is Brad interested in his education?" I asked skeptically.

"Don't know."

"Well, I know you're interested, so I wanted to let you know what's developing."

"Thanks."

We were silent and I couldn't think of anything else to say, so I supposed I'd have to go. I moved and Davy looked up at me, eyes and face sober.

"Don't be too hard on him," he said. "He's hard to deal with, I know, but there's a reason. Brad gets drunk ever' weekend, course you know that, ever' one does, but what most people don't know is Brad gets fed up an' disgusted with hisself, I guess, an' he takes it out on Luther. Always has, since he was a little boy. That's why I've sorta took a interest in him an' tried to help a little."

"No, I didn't know that. I'm sorry. If I'd known perhaps I could have been of more help to him. As it is, I feel I've failed to teach him or help him in any way at all."

"Wasn't your fault."

"Well, I'm glad you've told me, it's easier to cope when I know why the children do the things they do."

"There was a 'specially bad time right after you come here. You got th' backwash from that one an' blamed me."

He ended with a small quizzical grin in my direction. I gasped aloud.

"You mean it was because—? Oh, Davy, I'm sorry. All along I've been blaming you, thinking it was you—"

"S'all right. Might've been partly my fault."

He held out a closed hand to me. I automatically reached out and he dropped a thin shaving in the shape of a perfect ringlet in my hand. I looked at it lying there in my palm and was strangely touched. My hand closed carefully over it.

"So," Davy said. "You think it might be better if Luther had a job, instead of stayin' in school?"

"As a teacher, perhaps I shouldn't say it, but he's not doing any good in school. He's not doing anything at all, just sits there and stares out the window."

"Okay. I'll have a talk with John an' Brad, see what can be done. One thing I don't want is for him to repeat that little binge he had that time. Never was more surprised in all my life. That was th' one thing I never thought he'd ever get mixed up with."

"Perhaps it was a way of hitting back at his father. Did his parents ever find out about it?"

"No, don't think so."

"It might have been best if they had."

"Maybe, or maybe Brad woulda beat him within a inch of his life."

"He—does that?"

"Sometimes."

"I'm sorry I haven't been more understanding with him."

"Probably wouldn't made any difference."

He picked up the plane again and I guessed the interview was over.

"Well," I said slowly, "I guess I'd better go, I'm keeping you from your work. I just wanted you to know—about Luther."

"Okay."

I pulled my coat closer around my shoulders, the shaving curl still carefully enclosed in my hand and moved slowly toward the door. I felt strangely forlorn and dejected. At the door I turned. He was looking after me, an odd expression on his face. Our eyes held for a moment before I murmured good night and left. I walked slowly back to the house and spent the rest of the evening restlessly pacing the floor. I wrapped the little shaving in a tissue and put it at the back of one of my wardrobe drawers before I went to bed.

The week dragged on. I saw no more of Davy except at suppertime and then he had very little to say, but sometimes I would look up unexpectedly and catch his eyes on me with a strange intensity. He seemed unusually sober. I knew he was tired from the long hours he was working, and probably he was quite concerned about Luther. I thought about making another trip out to the shop to ask how things were developing there, but I didn't. I had the uneasy feeling that I might not be quite welcome.

CHAPTER TWENTY-NINE

Stuck!

*T*he weather was still drizzly but not freezing, it hadn't really rained hard all week. I hadn't been in town for three weeks, so on that Friday I decided on a sudden impulse to go. I'd gotten through all right that last time when Sue Proctor and her girls were with me and I didn't think the roads would be any worse now than they were then.

I hurried home from school, told Clemmy what I was going to do, and threw a few things in my suitcase. If I left right away, I could be through the tricky part of the road while it was still daylight. I also wanted to get away before Davy came home and tried to stop me.

Clemmy was worried and didn't think I should try it, but I was determined. I'd go mad if I had to be stuck in that cabin much longer.

The road was not particularly muddy but it was deeply rutted and slick. If I could just stay out of the ruts, I thought I'd be okay.

I got through the creek all right and up the next hill. I was breathing a sigh of relief when the back wheels suddenly slid sideways and pulled the front wheels into the deep ruts. I slid along that way for several feet, fighting to straighten the car and ended up crosswise in the road and firmly stuck. I couldn't go forward and I couldn't go back and every effort I made just put me in deeper.

I finally shut off the engine and just sat there trying to think what to do. Should I stay with the car or try to walk

171

back? I was probably a couple of miles from the Hilton's but only about a mile from the Anderson's. Either way I'd have to wade through the creek, and then I remembered I'd forgotten by boots. I was an idiot, plain and simple.

I sat there awhile, beginning to be afraid. It was Friday night and the men at the sawmill were paid on Friday and often went into town for a spree. Davy's brother Brad always did, and perhaps Tom too. A little bad weather wouldn't stop them, they'd go in by wagon and mule if necessary. I was wary of Brad Hilton and downright afraid of Tom. If he came, I didn't know what I'd do.

I shivered and locked the doors and wished I hadn't been so headstrong and foolish. Would Davy worry about me and come look for me?

It was growing dark and I had just about decided I'd have to get out and walk back or be prepared to spend the night in my car, when I saw headlights flickering in the distance, coming toward me. I sat up and watched—would it be Davy or someone else? I rolled my window down and recognized the sound of a tractor. It had to be Davy, he was the only one around here who had a tractor that I knew about. I was relieved but depressed, remembering what he'd said about always being the one who had to pull foolish women teachers out of ditches.

When he swerved the tractor around and jumped down I saw that it was Davy. He hauled out a heavy chain, hooked it to the back of the tractor and to my front bumper. I started my engine.

"Turn it off," he shouted. "Cramp your wheels to th' right 'til you're straight in th' road, then jist steer it."

I did as he said, biting my lip. He sounded angry and I didn't blame him. When the car was straight, my wheels went into the ruts and I guess that's the way he wanted it. I didn't even have to steer very much. He pulled me all the way to the house, then jumped down and unhooked the chain and drove the tractor off in the direction of the shed.

I got out of the car with my suitcase and went up to the house. Clemmy had waited up.

"I should have listened to you," I said despondently.

She patted my shoulder. "Maybe next week'll be better. There's some supper left hot on th' stove. Think I'll go on to bed."

"Good night."

I took my coat off and threw it across the bed, put my suitcase in the corner. I went back into the kitchen and looked in the pot on the stove. It was stew and it smelled delicious. I was very hungry, but just then Davy came in on a draft of cold air. I turned my back.

"I'm sorry," I said, my voice unsteady.

He didn't answer but a moment later his hands were on my shoulders, turning me. I looked up to see him grinning rather quizzically down at me. My lower lip trembled and hot tears rushed to my eyes.

"S'all right," he said gently. "Don't cry. You're runnin' 'bout par for th' course. Ever' teacher that comes out here does it at least once."

The tears were spilling down my cheeks and he put his arms around me and pulled me toward him and held me loosely. I sobbed, and suddenly overwhelmed by my loneliness, put my arms tight around him and drew as close to him as I could. He held me close while I shed a few tears on his chest. It felt so good to be near someone again.

After awhile his arms began to loosen and he held me away from him. I kept my head bowed while I searched for a handkerchief. He pulled out his shirttail and offered it to me. I gave a watery little giggle and wiped my tears away.

"It's always 'bout this time of year th' teacher starts throwin' herself at me too," he said with a lopsided grin.

"So you think I'm running pretty much true to type, do you?"

"Yep. Pretty much."

He tucked his shirttail back in, still looking at me.

"I'm surprised you don't flee the country," I said with an attempt at lightness.

"I've thought about it, 'specially in the past few weeks."

"I haven't bothered you the past few weeks, in fact I've hardly seen you."

"No, but th' way you've looked at me—"

"How have I looked at you?"

"Like a little girl lost. Like I'm your last hope. Sure has been temptin'. In fact, first time I ever was tempted by a teacher."

"I haven't been trying to tempt you," I said indignantly.

"Didn't mean that. Wash your face an' let's eat. I'm starved."

When we sat down to stew and cold corn bread and milk he spoke again.

"If you're a good girl, I might let you go into town with me tomorrow. I'm thinkin' of goin' in with th' truck."

"Why didn't you tell me?"

"When I got home you was gone. Jist decided this afternoon."

I sat and looked at my plate.

"Well?" he asked. "Want to go?"

"Yes, please."

"I'll probably stay th' night with John an' Carrie an' come back Sunday afternoon. That suit you?"

"Yes, that'll be fine."

"I'd like to get started 'bout nine in th' mornin'."

"Will—anyone else be going along?"

"Goldie, you mean? No."

"Oh."

"I only went out with her 'cause I was thinkin' too much about another girl an' I thought it might help, but it didn't."

"If you were thinking so much about the other girl, why didn't you ask her out?"

"Couldn't. She's not available."

"Oh," I said again. I had a sudden vision of Sue Proctor with her shining hair and her eyes lifted adoringly to Davy's face. It left a bad taste in my mouth. I hoped he hadn't gotten himself involved with her. It would be tragic for all of them.

"Eat your supper," he said. "Then I'll help wash up an' I might even stay an' play some cards with you."

"Why? Are you feeling sorry for me?"

"Heapin' coals of fire on your head," he answered with a grin, but not quite meeting my eyes.

CHAPTER THIRTY

Out on the Town

Next morning after breakfast I dressed in a plaid skirt and a soft blue long-sleeved blouse with ruffles at the neck. I used a little light makeup, something I hadn't bothered with for some time. I had put a few curlers in the front of my hair the night before and now as I brushed it, it curled closer to my face than usual.

My medium high-heeled shoes made me feel really dressed up. Out here I always wore low-heeled sturdy shoes for walking. I dabbed perfume behind my ears and stood back to view as much of myself as I could in the mirror. I was satisfied, and went into the kitchen. Davy was there waiting. He put his newspaper down and stood up and looked at me.

"Ready?" he asked.

"Ready."

I gave him a small impish grin. "You look nice," I said demurely.

"You don't look so bad yourself," he returned, unsmiling, but his eyes twinkled down on me.

I gave a mock sigh of resignation. "Ah, well. Who wants compliments anyway?"

"What can you expect from a backwoods hillbilly farmer?"

"You could say the blue of my blouse brings out the blue of my eyes, or you could say something about my shining waves of light brown hair."

"Get your coat. I want to get goin'."

I deliberately fluttered my eyelashes at him but he was unmoved. I went back in my room for my coat and the suitcase I had packed the afternoon before.

I stuck my head through the living room door. "Goodbye, Clemmy. Is there anything I can bring you from town?"

"No, I reckon not. Davy's got the grocery list."

"I meant for yourself."

"I don't need nothin'."

"Nevertheless, I'm going to get her a new corn bread pan," I said to Davy as we went out. "Do you know her old pan has a couple holes in it, so that I've seen her put the pan over the open fire and put a little corn bread in it to patch the holes before she pours the rest of it in?"

"No, I didn't know that."

"Your mother is the most self-sacrificing, unselfish person I've ever known. How long since she's been into town or had something new for herself? There must be lots of things she'd like to have yet when you ask her, she says not. How'd you ever deserve a mother like that?"

"Probably don't," he answered, opening the truck door for me. He helped me climb in, it was rather high, a ton and a half truck with extra big mud-grip tires. He put the suitcase in at my feet and closed the door. He came around to the other side, got in, started the truck and eased it into gear.

"Hang on to your hat," he said.

"I didn't wear a hat," I answered pertly.

"Afraid of messin' up your shinin' waves of light brown hair?"

"You noticed," I crowed, with mock delight.

He gave a quirk of a grin and concentrated on the muddy road. I withdrew into a rather vague type of daydreaming, until we drew near a home I had visited once.

"Have you heard anything about the Simpsons?" I asked.

"Nope. Heard they might've moved further back in th' hills."

"Wasn't it strange how they just disappeared without a trace? One day they were there, and the next day they were gone. Makes you wonder, doesn't it?"

He shrugged. "They come here th' same way, jist showed up one day, nobody knew how or from where."

"Strange. I can't help wondering what will become of those cute little girls."

We lapsed into silence again. At the end of the long muddy road and just before we reached the highway, he pulled over and stopped before a prosperous-looking brick farm house. This was the Miller place and they collected the mail for the Hiltons, as the mailman didn't attempt to travel the winding dirt roads even in summer.

"Jist as well get th' mail now," Davy said as he got out. He didn't say anything about me getting out too, so I stayed in the truck.

When he came back, he tossed two letters in my lap. I took them up and saw that one was from my mother and one was from Don. I glanced at Davy. He had started the truck and was looking around to the left to check before he pulled out into the road again.

I opened the letter from my mother. She was full of news about my sisters and a cousin who had recently become engaged, and light gossip about some of the neighbors. I folded the letter and put it back in the envelope. I hesitated a moment then put both letters into my purse.

"Ain't you gonna read your letter from your fella?"

"Not right now. I can't read too much when I'm traveling, it gives me a sort of motion sickness."

I felt him look at me but I kept my eyes on the road. We were silent the rest of the way into town.

Before we reached the business area Davy turned off into a side street.

"First thing I have to do is take some cabinets to John. Okay?"

I nodded.

"Want to come in for awhile? You could maybe phone your friends."

"Good idea."

He helped me down from the truck and we went up the walk together. John met us at the door.

While John and Davy unloaded the truck I went inside and used the phone. My friends were not home. Carrie offered me coffee and we sat down and made idle conversation. When the men came in, they joined us for a few minutes.

"Get hold of your friends?" Davy asked me presently.

"No, they're not home, but you can just drop me off somewhere downtown and I'll try calling them later," I said carefully, not meeting his eyes. "If they're still not home, I can call a taxi."

He nodded and put down his empty coffee cup. "All right if I stay here tonight?" he asked Carrie.

"Sure," she said and turned to me. "You can stay too, if you'd like. We have room."

"Thank you very much, but the Carters keep a room ready for me when I come into town."

"Ready?" Davy asked.

"Yes. Thanks for the coffee," I said to Carrie.

They came to the door and saw us off. I felt a little self-conscious for some reason when Davy helped me up into the truck.

"Your brother and his wife are nice people," I said for want of something better to say.

"Yes," he answered. "I stayed with them a year and went to ninth grade and learned a little about carpentering."

"You couldn't have stayed longer?"

"Got too durn homesick."

"You'll never live anywhere else, will you, Davy?"

"Don't think I could."

"I talked to Carrie once about Calvin staying with them so he could go to high school."

"She told me."

"Did she seem favorable? She's never mentioned it again to me. I don't even know if she mentioned it to John."

"She did, an' they'll have him if he wants to go an' if Granny'll let him."

"She'd better."

"What'll you do if she don't?"

"Nothing. I won't be here."

"John'll talk her around."

"You think so?"

"Yes."

"I'm glad. Calvin needs an education, he needs a chance to make a career for himself, maybe with his writing."

"Maybe you oughta stick around an' see that he does."

"I'll depend on you and John to do that."

We were silent as he drove the big mud-spattered truck carefully through the busy streets.

"Where do you want me to drop you?"

"Anywhere on the next corner will be all right," I answered, aware of a feeling of flatness within myself.

"If you wanted to, you could go on with me to the lumberyard, then we could stop somewhere for lunch, an' you could do your shopping after that."

"All right," I answered immediately. He looked surprised. "I don't really have all that much shopping to do," I added, feeling myself flush.

I got down and went inside the lumberyard with him while he chose the lumber he wanted and bought varnish and paintbrushes and nails.

"Where do you want to go to lunch?" he asked me then.

"Anywhere. A sandwich will be fine for me."

"Any special kind?"

"Barbecue? I've been hungry for a barbecue sandwich for weeks."

"There's a place not far from here where they make awful good barbecue sandwiches. Okay?"

"Okay."

We sat by a window where we could keep an eye on the truck and ate barbecue sandwiches and French fries and malts. We didn't have a lot to say to each other, there had been an odd kind of restraint between us ever since he had picked up the mail at Miller's. I sighed and wondered vaguely what Don had written about. I hadn't heard from him for some time.

"What's th' matter?" Davy asked. "Don't you like your sandwich?"

"It's delicious."

"Bored with th' company you're keepin' then?"

I smiled at him. "No, just thinking."

"About your letter?"

I nodded.

"Go ahead and read it. I won't look."

"There's no hurry," I said indifferently. "I mean—I'll read it later this evening."

He looked puzzled and curious but he didn't question me further. We finished our lunch and went back to the downtown area. Instead of dropping me off he found a place and parked the truck.

"Aren't you afraid someone might steal your things?" I asked.

"I'll put th' small stuff in th' cab and lock it up. Doubt if anyone'll carry off th' lumber in th' middle of town. Your suitcase should be all right."

I stood hesitant on the sidewalk while he transferred the things and locked up. Then he came over and we fell into step together.

"Where do you want to go first?" he asked.

"Are you coming with me?"

"Do you mind?"

"No, actually that would be nice. It's not much fun doing things alone."

We went inside several stores and looked around but

bought little. He bought a sack of lemon drops and shared them with me. We went around with bulging cheeks, laughing at each other. I bought some hose and a thick notebook for myself and one for Calvin. We looked a long time before we found a corn bread pan as big as the one Clemmy used and I insisted on paying for it in spite of Davy's protest. He bought a shirt after some deliberation and argument with me and then it was getting on toward evening.

"I'm getting hungry again," he said. "Let's go somewhere for supper."

"I should call my friends again." We found a pay phone. I dialed but still no answer.

"Let's get rid of these things and go find a place to eat."

"My feet hurt," I said.

"Th' price of vanity. You sit there on th' bench an' I'll take these things back to th' truck. Do you have some more sensible shoes in your suitcase?"

I sat down and put my feet out and looked at my shoes. "Yes, but—" I said reluctantly.

He grinned. "Okay, but I may end up carrying you, like I did that time you visited Granny Eldridge, remember?"

"Don't remind me."

"Don't run away. I'll be right back."

We had a leisurely supper together in a nice restaurant, then we decided to go on to a show. We saw a double feature, a Western and a love story. We ate popcorn and drank Coke, and both sat engrossed in the show. The theatre was crowded, of necessity we sat close, his arm against my shoulder. I was very aware of him and felt a little breathless when he moved a little once and looked down at me.

We lingered around town for awhile after we came out of the theatre, looking in shop windows, not talking much. It was one o'clock in the morning when he took me to my friends' home.

The house was dark. Davy walked up to the house with me.

"They must be out of town," I said.

"Want to come back with me? Carrie wouldn't mind."

"No, they said it was all right for me to stay even if they were gone. I have a key."

I unlocked the door and he came in with me. I switched on the living room light and went over to the telephone stand. There was a note for me.

"They've gone to visit relatives," I said, showing it to him.

"I don't like leavin' you here alone."

"I don't mind. I'll be all right."

"Okay. What time should I pick you up tomorrow?"

"What time do you want to get back?"

"Sometime in the afternoon, about three?"

"That's fine."

"I'll be here."

I went to the door with him. He turned, his hand on the knob and looked at me. I looked back and could think of nothing to say.

Finally he reached out and put his hand against my cheek.

"Good night. Call me if you need anything. Do you have John's phone number? I'll write it down."

He went back to the telephone pad and wrote down a number.

"Thanks for the meals and for the show," I said.

"I enjoyed it."

He was gone and I closed the door and stood there thoughtful. Then, though it was late, I went into the bathroom and ran water into the tub, and began to remove my clothes. Only then did I remember I'd left my suitcase in the truck.

CHAPTER THIRTY-ONE

Roller Skating

*T*he phone rang about nine the next morning while I was still asleep. I got up and padded into the living room in my slip.

"Hello."

"Anne?"

" 'Lo, Davy."

"Were you still sleepin'?"

"Um-mm. Did you cop my suitcase?"

"Sorry. Must'a had my mind on somethin' else. I'll bring it over now if you're up."

"Thank you. I'd appreciate that."

I didn't feel like putting on the same clothes I'd worn yesterday, so I borrowed a long bathrobe from my hostess and went to the kitchen to make coffee. I had brushed my hair and splashed water on my face when Davy knocked on the door.

"Come in," I said.

"Should I?" he asked.

"Shouldn't you? I've made coffee. Have you had breakfast?"

"Matter of fact, I haven't. Carrie was still in bed."

He came in and put my suitcase on the floor and looked around the room. It was beautifully and richly decorated and furnished.

"Sit down and I'll get you a cup of coffee."

I brought the coffee and set it on a coaster on an end table.

He sat down and looked up at me. I smiled, he was a little awkward in the elegant surroundings, and I felt quite tender toward him.

"If you'll wait while I get dressed, I'll fix breakfast for you."

I dressed in sweater and slacks, not bothering with makeup and went back to him.

"You don't mind if I wear slacks?"

His eyes traveled over me and back down to his cup.

"No," he said.

"I know your parents don't approve, so I don't wear them there, but I like to wear them when I come into town. Let's go see what we can scrounge up for breakfast."

The refrigerator was well stocked when I opened it.

"Bacon and eggs, sausage, pancakes?" I asked, looking over my shoulder.

"You can cook then?"

"Of course I can cook. Reasonably well too. Not like your mother, of course. I know—we'll have waffles. There's a waffle iron here somewhere."

I opened a can of orange juice and poured us each a glass. He stood leaning against the counter and watched me, sipping his juice.

"Bacon or sausage with your waffles?" I asked.

"Bacon."

"Don't you get enough bacon at home?"

"Yes, but it's different."

I looked at the thin strips and thought of the thick slabs of bacon Clemmy cooked. "You're right. Not better, just different. Well, sit down and take a load off your feet."

He pulled a chair out and sat down, but he still watched me. I felt very self-conscious.

The waffles were perfect, crisp and light. I served them with maple syrup and bacon. He ate four and pronounced them delicious.

I washed the dishes and he dried. When we went back into the living room I brought in the Sunday paper and we shared it and had more coffee.

"Know what I'd like to do this afternoon?" he said when he laid the paper aside.

"What?" I asked, stretching and yawning.

"Go roller skating. Do you like to skate?"

"I used to love it, but I haven't been for years."

"Then let's go, okay?"

"Would it be open today?"

"About three, I think."

"Thought you wanted to start home about then."

"There's no hurry, is there?"

"Not for me."

"Then?"

"Okay."

"Want to go anywhere before then?"

"Not especially."

"I have to stop at the grocery store for Mom but I can do that before we go skating. The skating rink is on the highway going home."

"Am I dressed okay?"

"Okay," he said and added, "I don't have anything to do before then. How about you?"

"Nothing. Not much going on today," I yawned again. "I stayed up and read last night. I was thinking of another long hot bath and maybe a nap."

"Guess I'll be going then. Thanks for breakfast."

"You're welcome. You'll be back about two-thirty or so then?"

"Yes, unless you'd want to come an' have lunch with me an' Carrie an' John?"

"No, I don't think so, Davy. Thanks anyhow. I think I'll just stay here and relax."

I took a long, scented bath and washed and set my hair. I

called my parents collect and talked a good while, then lay down for a short nap. Someone pounding on the door woke me. I looked at the clock and gasped. It was almost two-thirty. I pulled on my bathrobe and went to open the door. Davy was standing there, his look of concern changing to amusement.

"All ready and excited about goin' I see," he said dryly.

"Oh, Davy, I'm sorry. I didn't mean to sleep so long."

"Do I come in an' wait or go away an' come back?"

"Come in. It won't take me a minute."

"Says you."

I was pulling the big pink curlers out of my hair with one hand and with the other holding my robe together. He chuckled as he closed the door behind him.

"Careful," he said, "you'll pull it all out by the roots. Then how would I compliment you on your beautiful shinin' waves of light brown hair?"

"You wouldn't anyhow," I said, leaving him standing there as I went back to the bedroom.

I dressed quickly in the same slacks and sweater and the sensible shoes. My hair looked nice, it did shine. I had plenty of bouncy curl this time. I put on lipstick and a little eye shadow, dabbed perfume behind my ears, and was ready. I made the bed and took up my suitcase, purse and coat.

"I'm ready," I said.

"Congratulations."

"I should just write the Carters a note."

I sat down and wrote it and on second thought, added a P.S. to let them know Davy had come over and I had fixed breakfast for him. That was in case any of the neighbors felt inclined toward gossip.

"Okay, all set. Did you get the groceries?"

"Yes."

"Would you mind stopping at the florist for a few minutes? I'd like to get your mother a plant."

"Okay."

I picked out a beautiful small African violet in bloom and paid for it and carried it carefully out to the truck. Davy got out to let me in on his side. He had put the box of groceries on the seat on my side, so that I had to sit in the middle.

"Pretty," he said.

"Isn't it? It's so delicate. I think your mother will like it."

"I know she will. You're good to her."

"I do very little for her compared to what she does for me."

"I'm glad you get along so well. It's good for Mom, havin' you around. You like it out there fairly well, don't you?"

"Yes, except for two things, snakes in summer and the loneliness in winter."

"Snakes don't usually bother us much an' if you was married an' had a family, you wouldn't be lonely."

"Sometimes married people are the most lonely in the world."

"Shouldn't be."

"No."

We lapsed into silence until he pulled into the parking lot at the skating rink. We could hear the music even out there, and I began to feel excited. It would be fun being on roller skates again. I jumped down after Davy, not realizing until I landed that my right foot had gone to sleep. The varnish and nails and my suitcase were all on the floor of the cab on my side and my foot had been rather cramped. I grabbed at Davy to support myself.

"Oh-h-h," I said.

"What's wrong? Hurt yourself?"

"My foot's gone to sleep."

"Well, jump around on it a little," he advised.

"Heartless brute," I returned. "If you were at all chivalrous you'd express proper concern and carry me in."

"Want me to?" he challenged.

"No, I don't."

"Well, make up your mind."

I let go of him and began hobbling toward the building, my head in the air. He chuckled.

Inside it was bright and cheery. The music was lively, the skaters whirled round and round the floor. There were not too many people yet, but it was filling up fast.

"What size?" Davy asked me.

"Six."

He left me standing at the rail. When he came back I sat down and reached for the skates. He put them on the floor and knelt before me and untied my shoe.

"I can do it," I said coolly.

"So can I."

He removed my shoe and began to gently massage my right foot."

"Better?" he asked in a minute, looking up at me.

I nodded and he put the shoe skate on me. He removed my other shoe and put the other skate on.

"You lace them up. I might get them too tight."

He rose from his knees and sat down beside me to put his own skates on. I laced and tied mine and rose to totter uncertainly over to the rail. It had been so long. Had I forgotten?

I clung to the rail for the first few minutes, then struck out on my own. I was going round for the second time before some of my confidence began to return and I began to move more smoothly. I began to free up and enjoy myself.

I saw Davy come out onto the floor out of the corner of my eye. He skated well with no apparent effort or self-consciousness. He passed me, not even looking my way. When I saw him again a woman with short dark hair was skating beside him talking and laughing and he was smiling in his rather sober way. I averted my eyes, and felt my lips tighten. "If that's the way he wants it, it's fine with me," I told myself. Nevertheless, I felt a little forlorn.

By this time I was skating naturally, not even thinking of

my feet. I was sober, my thoughts turned inward. When hands came around my waist, I looked up and Davy was behind me.

"Hi," he said.

I permitted myself a small smile and looked away.

"Mad at me?" he asked.

"Why should I be?"

"Don't know. Don't think I understand women very well."

He came along beside me, his right arm around my waist and reached for my left hand with his left. I put my right hand on his at my waist and we skated that way for several rounds until they cleared the floor. We sat down together, both of us silent, and watched all the children under twelve swarm out on the floor. Then it was "all skate" again and we rose together.

He stayed with me the rest of the time. We experimented with a few dance steps and tried skating backward, but mostly we just skated together in silence.

We had a supper of hot dogs, Cokes, and candy bars, then left for home about eight o'clock.

"That was fun," I said. "I'm glad you thought of it. Thank you."

"Thanks for goin' with me."

I leaned my head back on the seat while we drove toward home. It grew warm in the cab so I slipped my arms out of my coat and just kept it across my shoulders.

Once out on the muddy roads, I had to sit up and hang on. I was flung up against Davy more than once before he stopped at the edge of the yard.

He turned off the engine and the lights and sat for awhile with both hands on the wheel, very still. The moonlight streamed in through the window and his face looked almost stern. My heart was beating up in my throat. I told myself there was no point in making a move to get out until he did, because I was blocked in.

He turned and looked at me. His hands came up and pushed the coat off my shoulders, one hand slid down between the seat and my back.

"I always expect a good-night kiss when I take a girl out on the town," he said.

"Do you?"

"Yes."

I felt the warmth of his hand on my back and shivered. His other hand came over to my right shoulder and turned me toward him. I lifted my face and he leaned forward and kissed me.

"Put your arms around me, sweetheart," he whispered.

I put my arms up around his neck and he drew me closer. We kissed again, long and sweet and heart stopping.

"We'd better go in," I whispered presently.

His arms tightened, his mouth against my cheek, his heart thudding against me. "Not yet," he whispered. "Jist a minute longer, please, sweetheart."

He found my mouth again, and a little frightened, I pushed against him. He released me then and helped me back into my coat. I was shaking but not because of the cold, and I knew he was aware of it.

He got out and reached a hand out to help me down. We went around the truck together, not speaking. He gathered up my purchases and handed them to me, then took up the box of groceries himself and we went up to the house.

Inside, he put the box on a chair and turned to build up the fire. I went into my room and laid my purchases on the bed, the plant on my desk. I removed my coat, and hung it up and stood there irresolute before I went back into the kitchen.

We stood across the room looking at each other. My heart fluttered in my breast. I felt almost lightheaded.

"Thanks for—the weekend," I said with difficulty.

He nodded and suddenly I was filled with longing to feel his arms around me again. I went over to him and he gathered me close. My arms went up around his neck but almost immediately he released me and reached up to pull my arms away.

He turned and left me standing there and went out of the house.

CHAPTER THIRTY-TWO

The Heart of Me

Davy wasn't at breakfast next morning which was not terribly unusual. Sometimes he had his breakfast early, but I hadn't heard him come in. I hadn't slept well and was up early. It was hard to define my feelings even to myself, I seesawed back and forth between elation and sober reflection. I kept telling myself it meant nothing, just a good-night kiss or two and I'd had my share of good-night kisses, so what was so different about last night? Then the conviction that something momentous had happened to me would return and I'd experience that breathless feeling of elation again.

I gave Clemmy the new corn bread pan and the plant. She was touchingly pleased about both. I went on to school and fought with myself all morning to keep my mind on my business. By afternoon I had succeeded fairly well, but near time for school to be dismissed, I found my thoughts on Davy again, wondering if he might come and walk home with me as he'd done a few times in the past.

There was no sign of him and I walked home alone. He didn't come in to supper either. I ate but I didn't have much appetite.

"Where's Davy?" I finally asked Clemmy.

"He went to work on Jim's house. Said he might not be back 'til late."

"Oh."

Clemmy and Mr. Hilton had gone to bed, and still Davy

didn't come. I kept going to the window, but there was no light in the shop. I sat down and stared at my hands, unable to get interested in my schoolwork.

He came in on a rush of cold air at about ten o'clock, carrying an armload of wood. He dumped it into the wood box and took his coat off. He didn't look at me.

"Hello," I said. "I was wondering when you were going to come in. It's getting cold out, isn't it?"

He nodded, but didn't speak as he turned to hang his coat and hat on the nail by the door. He gathered up some firewood and went into the living room. I heard him building up the fire in there.

"Davy," I said when he came back, "is—something wrong?"

"No, nothin's wrong."

I swallowed. "Are you angry with me?"

I rose and went around to face him. He lifted his head and looked at me. I was shocked that his face was so haggard.

"Davy," I said again, uncertainly. I reached out and put my hand on his arm, but he removed it.

"Don't do that," he said gently.

"Don't do what? Davy, are you sick?"

"No, jist tired. It's been a long day. I jist came in a minute to build up th' fires."

"Why don't you sleep here tonight? The fire has probably gone out in the shop and it's cold."

"No."

"But—" I stopped as he reached out for his coat. "Can't you stay a little while? Did you have any supper? There's still some coffee hot on the stove."

"Jist leave me alone, can't you?"

I stepped back, surprised and hurt. He stood there looking at me, his face white and strained. The coat fell to the floor, he stepped over it and reached out and pulled me into his arms.

"I'm sorry," he groaned, straining me close. "I wasn't meanin' that. Aw, Anne, what am I gonna do?"

I was startled and tried to pull away, but he held me convulsively closer.

"Don't pull away from me, Anne," he whispered. "I've kept it all inside for so long. I can't fight it anymore. I tried so hard not to fall in love with you, but I couldn't seem to stop myself. Put your arms around me, please."

I put my arms up around his neck and hid my face in his shoulder. He put his head down against mine.

"You was so sweet this weekend," he said. "I knew I shouldn't take you with me but I wanted to. I thought maybe one time wouldn't hurt, but it finished me off for good. You're th' one woman I want in th' world an' I can't have you. That's hard, sweetheart, awful hard. You don't know how I've been tempted to try to make you love me an' forget about him."

"Davy."

"Don't say anything, little one. I don't want you to feel guilty, it ain't your fault. You're a long way from him an' you've been lonely, an' I've been th' only one around to talk to. You don't know how I been tempted to take advantage of that, but I tried not to. I've always tried to be honorable, but—"

He paused and I found I couldn't say a word.

"I know you've cared for me a little, but I know it's jist 'cause you're lonely. You'll forget me when you get back to him, but I'll never be able to forget you. You're right in th' very heart of me, in my blood and in my brain. There's not a minute I'm not thinkin' of you. I'll have to go away. I've been walkin' all afternoon, tryin' to make myself go away without seein' you again, but I wasn't strong enough. I had to see you, hold you one more time—"

He held me crushed against him, then released me so abruptly I had to grab hold of the back of a chair.

" 'Bye, Anne. Don't think too bad of me. I've valued your friendship."

"Davy, wait."

"It's no good, sweetheart. It wouldn't be right for me to stay. I couldn't keep away from you."

He picked up his coat and hat and was gone before I could say anything. I sat down in the chair, feeling weak and limp.

CHAPTER THIRTY-THREE

The Proposal

I spent three days arguing with myself, even aloud sometimes as I walked to and from school. Being alone so much in the evenings had done that to me.

"You idiot," I told myself. "Think of all your plans, your ambitions. You don't want to get mixed up with Davy Hilton."

"Oh, but I do, I do," an inner voice cried out.

"He's a country hillbilly," I continued on firmly. "While you've been city born and bred. What about your family, your friends, your plans to travel, see the country, maybe even teach in a foreign land? You think Davy Hilton will ever leave these hills? He's a part of them and they're a part of him. You heard him say he couldn't even stay away a year. Do you want to be stuck in the sticks for the rest of your life, not even being able to get into town sometimes for months at a time?"

"Oh, but it's beautiful here," my other self said. "So peaceful and quiet and serene."

In my bed at night I continued my musings, arguing back and forth, until I'd drop into an uneasy sleep of exhaustion.

"His grammar is atrocious," I thought. "Can I accept that, and not be continually correcting him, like the schoolteacher I am?"

"But," the other side said, "his grammar is quite good at times. That time Mr. Hooper was here and they talked, I was pleasantly surprised. If he could be in close contact with someone who used good grammar all the time, his would improve."

"Would you be uncomfortable, presenting him to your family and friends?"

"Mom liked him. Last weekend in town, women and girls looked at him and admired him. He's very striking, and kind. He's a lot like his mother that way, not like his father, or his brothers Brad and Tom. He has a keen sense of humor, he'd be popular wherever he went. Look how everyone looks up to him here."

"Would you want him to be the father of your children?"

"Yes."

There was no argument on that question. Davy was definitely good father material, I knew that by the way he treated his nieces and nephews, the way they loved and respected him.

On Friday morning, I knew I'd have to at least talk to him. He'd said he tried to be honorable. Well, I tried too, and I didn't want him thinking I'd let one man kiss me while I was committed to another. I at least had to explain that much to him. Before I left for school I went to his mother.

"Clemmy, do you know where Davy is? I want to talk to him. Can you give him a message for me?"

"I reckon I might."

"Just tell him I need to talk to him, will you? It's—important."

She treated me as always, but I couldn't help wondering what Davy had told her, and if he'd told her the truth, did she feel any resentment toward me? She had to get up to a cold house because there was no Davy to come in late and early and keep the fires going. I didn't know if she brought the firewood in or not, but I helped out some there. Mr. Hilton was doing the milking and feeding, he was home all that week for a change. Someone was still building up the fire at school early each morning.

My message brought results. While I was clearing off my desk after school that afternoon, Davy walked in. He looked hollow-eyed and tired, his body tense. I sat down in my chair, suddenly limp.

"Hello, Davy," I said with at least an appearance of calm.

"Mom said you wanted to talk to me."

"Yes, please. Sit down, won't you?"

"I don't have much time. Is it Luther?"

"No," I said shortly, "it's not Luther. It's me."

He came slowly around my desk, hat in hand and sat down on the bench.

"What about you?" he asked carefully.

"There's something I wanted to explain to you," I said stacking my papers on my desk, my eyes lowered. "You—you left so quickly the other night I didn't get a chance—"

"Tell me then."

I moistened my lips, still busy with the papers. "I'll—have to go back to when I first came here to make you understand. A—a young woman alone has to be careful, especially a teacher. People expect—well you know a teacher has to have a good reputation, you said that yourself, so—"

I stopped and he waited. I plunged on again.

"You were leery of me because of what happened with the teacher last year, and then your brother Tom brought his kids to school a couple of times and he—well, I didn't like his attitude and the way he looked at me. It scared me a little. Then Jim tried to involve me in his problems, so to protect myself I told you that I had no interest in any of you, that I was more or less committed, I had someone waiting for me in St. Louis."

"You mean it ain't true?"

I shook my head. "It wasn't really a lie. I did have someone waiting for me. You met him, Don Bradford, at your mother's family get-together."

"You broke up with him?"

"No. He asked me to marry him before I came out here. I

said no, but he said I might change my mind and he'd wait. So you see, it wasn't really a lie."

"Why didn't you tell me?"

"I tried to, but you ran off before I could."

"I mean before that."

"There wasn't really an opportunity. I couldn't just walk up and say 'there's no one I'm committed to, Davy.' That would have been like—"

"Why couldn't you?"

I felt a little put out. "I wasn't sure I wanted to," I said, a bit truculent.

"Then why are you tellin' me now?"

"Because I wanted—I didn't want you to think I'd let one man make love to me while I was committed to another. I try to be an honorable person too."

He put his hat on his head, rose and came to me. He grasped my upper arms and almost jerked me to my feet, his jaw clamped, his eyes steely gray.

"You let him kiss you," he said.

"Who?"

"Don what's-his-name."

"Yes, I did. He's not the first man who's kissed me by a long shot."

"Do you love me?"

"I—don't know."

"Are you playin' with me by any chance? Jist another notch in your belt?"

"I am not. Davy, you know I wouldn't do that."

"I don't know anything anymore."

He pulled me against him and almost crushed me, his mouth came down on mine and kissed me savagely. When he put me away from him he looked grim and hard.

"Either you love me, or you don't," he said harshly. "Either you want to marry me an' give up all them other men, or you don't."

"What other men?" I cried wildly.

"I'm goin' back to Jim's but I'll be back in a couple days. Make up your mind."

"I don't need a couple of days to make up my mind," I cried after him. "I can give you your answer right now and it's no!"

He didn't stop, and I sat down again and felt my face pucker.

"Oh, darn," I said, and pounded my fist on the desk. I sat there a minute, then let my head sink down onto my arms, a few tears squeezed out of my eyes.

I couldn't have sat there more than a minute or two when I felt his big hand on my head. I looked up and he was on one knee beside my chair, his hat on the back of his head, his face gentle and contrite.

"I'm sorry, sweetheart," he said quietly. "I had no right to treat you like that. I know I shouldn't make excuses, but th' past few weeks have been hell, an' I was hurt 'cause you didn't tell me before 'bout that fella in St. Louis. Will you forgive me, please?"

I nodded, biting my lower lip to stop it trembling. I put my arms around his neck and pressed my face into his shoulder. He picked me up and sat down in my chair with me on his lap. His hat fell off and landed on the floor behind us.

"My little love, you don't know how hard it's been, knowin' you was up there at th' house, alone an' lonely. Lots of times I started up there an' turned around halfway an' went back, knowin' I couldn't be with you like that an' keep my hands off you. I fell awful deep in love with you, but knowin'—" he paused and corrected himself, "thinkin' you was belongin' to someone else, I couldn't do anything about it. Jist now when you told me there never had been anyone else, it made me feel—I've done a awful lot of hurtin' over you lately an' you must've known how I was feelin'. It hurt that you didn't tell me sooner."

"But I didn't know, Davy. I had no idea. I thought—"

"You didn't know?" he asked lifting my face and making me look at him. "But how could you not know?"

"I didn't, Davy, how could I? You never said anything."

"I thought I said enough."

"It's very hard sometimes to tell when you're serious and when you're teasing, Davy, and I thought—"

"You thought what?"

"I thought you were attracted to Sue Proctor."

His mouth literally fell open, he looked stunned, then he pushed me off his lap and stood up, swooping on his hat and jamming it back on his head.

"Say that again," he said slowly, incredulously.

"I thought—well, why shouldn't I think it? That first day when you came home and I'd washed her hair, you couldn't take your eyes off her. You let her come and clean up for you and you wouldn't let me. She's been to the house you're building and you've never invited me even to come see it."

"You sound like a jealous wife," he said softly. "I looked at her, sure, she was like a different person. I let her clean up because it needed it an' she needed th' money, an' she comes to th' house I'm buildin' once in awhile 'cause her husband is there. I didn't invite you 'cause I didn't know you'd be interested, an' I was tryin' to stay away from you."

I sniffed rather disdainfully and reached for my purse. I fished in it for a tissue and the letter I'd received from Don came to the surface. I'd forgotten all about it. Davy reached over my shoulder and plucked it out of my bag.

"You never even opened it," he said slowly.

"I forgot about it," I answered drying my eyes.

He held the letter over the wastebasket and let it drop. I replaced the tissue and closed my purse. We eyed each other from a distance of a few feet.

"You explain to me what you meant by 'all them other men' I'm to give up," I said and it was his turn to look uncomfortable.

"Jim's back, an' Tom was over an' they—"

"They have no right to talk about me in that way," I said angrily. "They have absolutely no basis for it, and you shouldn't let them."

"They only was sayin' how cute you are an'—an' all. It made me think you could have jist about any man you wanted, an' then you said you'd kissed lots of men, an' it made me see red."

"I didn't say I'd kissed lots of men exactly, I just—oh, well, you know how it is. Kisses don't necessarily mean anything."

"Do to me."

"As for your friend Jim Baker, I don't think I like him much in spite of his winning ways. I'm going to give him a piece of my mind next time I see him. And your brother Tom, with his roving eyes and his little affairs. I don't see why Ellen stays married to him."

"She ain't."

"She ain't? I mean she isn't? Is she getting a divorce?"

"I shouldn't've said that. Don't say anything, will you? She ain't getting a divorce, jist ain't married to him. Never has been."

"Not—married?" I said aghast. "But then why does she stay with him?"

" 'Cause of the kids, an' 'cause she loves him. Don't ask me why, I don't understand it either. Don't say anything, I don't think even th' kids know."

I was silent, appalled. That nice woman, Ellen, to have to live like that.

"And your father accepts his kids but not Calvin," I said with a touch of bitterness. "Now that's ironic."

"Ain't it though?"

"I would never put up with a man like that, like Tom, I mean."

"No reason why you should, at least, not if you marry me."

"Who says I'm going to marry you?"

"No one," he said meekly, then added, "yet."

"And I could never, ever fetch and carry for a man the way your mother does for your father."

"No?" he asked with a little grin. He came over to me and put his hands on my shoulders. He bent and brushed his lips across my cheek, his arms went around me.

"Davy," I said weakly. "We have to talk."

"Who wants to talk?" he murmured against my mouth.

"I do."

He kissed me, then released me with a sigh.

"Okay, teacher, start talkin'."

I seated myself on the bench, my hands in my lap. He came over and sat down a few feet distant and removed his hat, turning it around and around by the brim, studying it. He made me think of an uneasy, unsure schoolboy, and I wasn't sure if it was intentional or not.

"Davy, I've had so many plans, so many things I wanted to do."

He was still turning the hat around and around. It irritated me. I reached over and snatched it out of his hand and put it down on the other side of me.

"Hey, be careful with my hat."

"Look at me when I'm talking to you," I snapped.

"Yes, ma'am."

I had to laugh. "Oh, Davy, you don't want to marry me," I said almost tearfully.

"Don't I?" he returned, his eyes warm and smiling.

"I'm bossy and hard to get along with. I'd be trying to tell you what to do, correcting your grammar, nagging you about your tenses. I'm not the submissive type. I have ideas and opinions and I'm used to getting my way a lot, none of this keeping her pregnant and barefoot for me."

"You're all I ever wanted," he said quietly.

I bit my lip and blinked my eyes. His hand came over and rested on my shoulder, his fingers gently caressing.

"Davy, could I—could we wait until spring to get married—" I stopped, appalled.

"What's wrong?"

"Did you—I don't know if you did ask me to marry you," I said in little more than a whisper.

"I did."

"Oh."

"Want me to ask you again?"

He slid closer and put his arm around me and murmured against my hair, words of love, sweet and thrilling. I was trembling when he raised his head and put his hand under my chin.

"Little one, will you marry me?" he asked softly.

"Davy, that's not fair. I can't think straight."

"Don't think, jist say yes."

I pulled away from him and rose.

"Davy, all my life I've wanted to be a teacher, wanted to travel. You're asking me to give that all up for you."

"Not much of a bargain," he said solemnly, "but I love you an' I need you. I know I ain't good enough for you, but if you won't marry me, I'm gonna be miserable th' rest of my life, an' that's no joke. You wouldn't want to ruin my life, would you?"

"You'd recover."

"No."

Just that one word impressed me more than all the others. A sudden rush of tenderness for him filled me. I went and sat back down beside him.

"Davy."

"What, love?"

"You really do love me and want to marry me?"

"I really do."

"And—and you think we'd be happy together?"

"I do. Least I know I'd be th' happiest an' luckiest man in th' world."

"Perhaps if I went home for awhile when school is over I'd be in a better position to decide."

"No."

"No?"

"You have to decide now."

"I don't like ultimatums, Davy Hilton."

"If you go back to th' city, I'll lose you."

"You don't know that."

"I'm afraid of it. No, you have to decide now while th' balance is a little in my favor."

"But that's selfish."

"I know."

"But Davy, wouldn't it be better to find out now than after we were married?"

"No. Once you're mine, I'll keep you. If you went away and stayed away, I'd bring you back if I had to go to th' ends of th' earth. I might not be able to do that if we wasn't married."

I was silent. His hand came over and took hold of mine and turned it palm up.

"Such a little hand to hold all my happiness in it," he said thoughtfully. He lifted it and pressed a kiss into it, then closed my fingers over the kiss, one by one. My heart was fluttering in my throat, threatening to choke me.

"We'll have to live with Mom and Dad for awhile," he continued on. "But we'll be alone in th' evenin's. I'll build us a log cabin in that long valley south of Mom an' Dad, close enough so we can keep a eye on them when they get older, but not so close th' kids'll bother them with their noise."

"What kids?"

"Our kids, yours an' mine. You won't mind a log cabin, will you? Any other kind don't seem right in these hills somehow."

"You're taking an awful lot for granted, aren't you?"

"Mom can teach you about gardenin' an' cannin' an' all, an' we can maybe buy a little more land, do a little more farmin', besides my cabinet makin', so I can be home more an' we can be together."

"What about my teaching?"

"You can finish out this year, maybe even teach again next year, but I don't wanna wait too long before we start our own family."

"And may I ask when the wedding is going to take place?" I asked dryly.

" 'Bout two weeks, maybe three, I thought."

"Oh, you did, did you?"

"Yep."

"Well, for your information, I have no intention—"

He lunged forward and grabbed me and stopped me with his mouth on mine. I struggled for a minute but he held me tight. He kissed my cheeks and my eyes and hair, murmuring to me, his arms gentle but firm. I gave up and threw my arms around his neck and kissed him back.

"Oh, Davy, I love you."

"That's better. Thought you'd never give in. Now say you're gonna marry me."

"All right, Davy, I'll marry you."

"Next week?"

"But I thought you said I could have two or three weeks."

"I was jist thinkin', there's a holiday comin' up an' school's out for a week or so, ain't it? If we got married, say next Friday, we could have a honeymoon in town, all to ourselves, before you had to come back to teachin' an' me to my work. I'd like that jist fine, wouldn't you?"

"Oh, Davy, you're impossible."

"Might be able to improve me, if we was married."

"If we 'were' married, Davy, not 'was.' "

"If we were married. See? I'm improvin' already."

"You idiot."

"Is that any way to talk to your future husband?" he asked plaintively. He released me and drew back a little and looked at me, almost shamefaced.

"Sweetheart, I'm downright 'shamed of myself, throwin' my weight around, orderin' an' demandin' my own way 'bout everything, but if you'll jist let me have my way in two things, you can have all th' rest your way, I promise."

"What two things?"

"Marry me now, an' live with me here."

"Why does it have to be now? Why not in the spring when—"

" 'Cause I need you now. Th' nights are long an' cold an' lonely. In th' spring, I'll be busy, buildin' our house, plowin' an' plantin'. Spring's a busy time for a farmer, sweetheart, he don't have time for honeymoonin' then."

"You're trying to stampede me."

"Um-huh."

"Oh, all right, but my folks will have a fit. They've always pictured me in white satin with a long veil."

He looked troubled. "I wasn't thinkin' 'bout that."

"It's all right, Davy. I've never seen myself that way. I've always thought a wedding should basically be a private thing between a man and a woman, with maybe just a few close relatives or friends included."

"You're sure?"

"I'm sure."

"Then we'll go in tomorrow an' get th' blood tests an' license an' whatever an' be married next week?"

"Next Saturday, about two in the afternoon? Would that suit you, Mr. Hilton?"

He eyed me a little apprehensively. "You're not—not jist—"

"Not what?"

"You're takin' it too calm, too. You're worryin' me, makin' me wonder if you're meanin' any of this. You wouldn't do that to me, would you?"

"Of course not, Davy. And you say you want me to live here with you?"

He nodded, his eyes still wary.

"I'll agree to that too."

"You will? No fightin', no arguin' even?"

"Not at all," I said complacently. "I don't intend to be that kind of wife. You see, I don't have to be. You said if I agreed to these two conditions I could have everything else my way. Let's see, I'll want a large house, three or four bedrooms, with electricity and plumbing and a big fireplace in the living room, an electric range for cooking, and an electric washing machine. I'll want to take an extended trip every summer, perhaps to Europe, the Hawaiian Islands, perhaps a cruise on one of those luxury liners. I want a car or truck or whatever with a four-wheel drive so I can go into town just whenever I take the notion, a maid to wait on me, a white poodle to sit on my lap, a private swimming pool."

I stopped and gave a gurgle of laughter at the look on his face.

"Anything I've forgotten?" I inquired innocently.

"Might be somethin' in that keepin' her pregnant an' barefooted idea after all."

"Not for me, Davy Hilton."

"Well," he said softly, grinning, "not all th' time, anyway."

"Perhaps not any of the time," I said, putting my chin in the air.

"How you gonna have gran'kids if you don't have kids first, Mrs. Hilton?"

"Grandkids?"

"You said you're storin' up memories to share with your gran'kids, remember?"

"Oh, well—I didn't necessarily mean—that's just a figure of speech."

"Huh-uh. You're gonna have kids of your own, teacher, my kids."

He came over and knelt on one knee beside me again, his face very close and very tender. Touched and self-conscious, I looked down at my hands.

"A son," he said softly. "Ever' man wants a son, an' then a whole houseful of little girls exactly like their mama."

"Not a whole houseful, Davy, maybe two or three, but not a houseful. I do want to teach again. Perhaps before the children or after or—or even in between, but I don't want to give up teaching entirely. Will you agree to that?"

He nodded, his hand over mine. I had raised my eyes and was looking into his. I was trembling a little. I leaned forward and put my arms around him, my head on his shoulder.

"Oh, Davy. I want to tell you something. I shouldn't perhaps, you're bossy enough already, but I do love you so much. I've never, ever felt this way before. I didn't even know it was possible. When I was making all those plans for the future, they seemed so important, so—so vital, and now I'd give them all up in a minute for you. Even teaching if I have to, even my very life itself."

He held me tight, not saying a word, very still. I raised my head, and saw big tears slipping silently down his cheeks.

"Why, Davy, what's wrong?" I asked, alarmed.

"Nothin'."

He buried his face in my lap, his hands holding on to me. I took his hat off and stroked his hair, my heart full of tenderness for this big strong man who was suddenly weak in his need for me.

"I didn't let myself even think you could feel like that about me," he said presently, his voice muffled.

"But I can. I do, Davy. I want to be with you, always. The nights have been cold and long and lonely for me too. I've just realized what my problem has been these past few weeks. I haven't just been lonely, I've been lovesick."

"Me too."

He raised his head and smiled at me, wiping the backs of his hands across the dampness on his face. He rose to his feet and pulled me up after him.

"Let's go home an' tell Mom," he said.

THE END